THE
GREEK TYCOON'S
UNEXPECTED WIFE

BY
ANNIE WEST

⊚ ™ MILLS & BOON ®
Pure reading pleasure

DID YOU PURCHASE THIS BOOK WITHOUT A COVER?

If you did, you should be aware it is **stolen property** as it was reported *unsold and destroyed* by a retailer. Neither the author nor the publisher has received any payment for this book.

All the characters in this book have no existence outside the imagination of the author, and have no relation whatsoever to anyone bearing the same name or names. They are not even distantly inspired by any individual known or unknown to the author, and all the incidents are pure invention.

All Rights Reserved including the right of reproduction in whole or in part in any form. This edition is published by arrangement with Harlequin Enterprises II BV/S.à.r.l. The text of this publication or any part thereof may not be reproduced or transmitted in any form or by any means, electronic or mechanical, including photocopying, recording, storage in an information retrieval system, or otherwise, without the written permission of the publisher.

This book is sold subject to the condition that it shall not, by way of trade or otherwise, be lent, resold, hired out or otherwise circulated without the prior consent of the publisher in any form of binding or cover other than that in which it is published and without a similar condition including this condition being imposed on the subsequent purchaser.

® and TM are trademarks owned and used by the trademark owner and/or its licensee. Trademarks marked with ® are registered with the United Kingdom Patent Office and/or the Office for Harmonisation in the Internal Market and in other countries.

First published in Great Britain 2007
Harlequin Mills & Boon Limited,
Eton House, 18-24 Paradise Road, Richmond, Surrey TW9 1SR

© Annie West 2007

ISBN: 978 0 263 86398 7

Set in Times Roman 10½ on 12 pt
01-0108-51904

Printed and bound in Spain
by Litografia Rosés, S.A., Barcelona

Annie West spent her childhood with her nose between the covers of a book—a habit she retains. After years preparing government reports and official correspondence she decided to write something she *really* enjoys. And there's nothing she loves more than a great romance. Despite her office-bound past she has managed a few interesting moments—including a marriage offer with the promise of a herd of camels to sweeten the contract. She is happily married to her ever-patient husband (who has never owned a dromedary). They live with their two children amongst the tall eucalypts at beautiful Lake Macquarie, on Australia's east coast. You can e-mail Annie at www.annie-west.com

MORAY COUNCIL LIBRARIES & INFO.SERVICES	
20 23 74 98	
Askews	
RF	

To Tessa.
For taking a chance on me,
for your support, advice and encouragement, and
for your generosity in sharing your name for this story!
Thank you.

CHAPTER ONE

STAVROS DENAKIS surveyed the crowd spilling out from his villa and permitted himself a single satisfied smile.

The engagement party was perfect. As planned.

It was a superb evening for a celebration. The black velvet of the Aegean sky shone with a lustrous net of stars and a light breeze tempered the heat.

The murmurs and laughter of delighted guests rose above a discreet background of live music. The crates of iced vintage champagne emptied almost as quickly as they were supplied.

Unerringly Stavros located his father's wheelchair on the flagged terrace nearest the house. The old man wore a rare smile as he chatted with one of his cronies. Even from this distance his renewed vigour was obvious.

Yes. Stavros had made the right decision with tonight's announcement.

Dispassionately he watched Angela walk down the wide stairs to the second terrace, drawing attention even among the crowd of wealthy, beautiful people. She was poised and elegant, wearing with apparent nonchalance the collar of diamonds he'd given her. There was just enough sway in those sleekly rounded hips to hold a sensual promise. For the right man.

The perfect fiancée.

She joined a cluster of guests who were neither relatives nor close friends. They were business associates.

Angela understood the value of these new associates to his latest expansion. Not indispensable to him: no one was that. But useful, worth time and effort. Already she was charming the group with her beauty and attentive interest.

She had just the right blend of wit and good looks. Of intelligence and sensuality. Of spirit and acquiescence to his wishes.

She would make the perfect wife for the CEO of Denakis International.

'Kyrie Denakis.'

He swung round to see his head of security approaching.

Stavros registered mild annoyance. There must have been yet another attempted press intrusion. A major one this time, for Petros to bother him with it now.

For weeks his staff had repelled attempts by the paparazzi to find a way into tonight's celebration. It had even been necessary to enforce a blanket no-fly zone over the island to ensure privacy.

'Is there a problem?'

A ripple of expression crossed Petros' features, a fleeting look of unease. That in itself was unique. Immediately Stavros stiffened, alert to the fact that something was most definitely wrong.

'We have a…situation, *kyrie.*'

He nodded. That much was obvious.

'A young woman has arrived.'

What had she done? Broken her neck attempting to scale the perimeter wall? Half-drowned herself trying to swim ashore unseen? Whatever her actions, the results were serious judging by the almost-expression on Petros' dour features.

'And?'

'She is demanding to see you.'

For an instant Stavros felt his eyes widen in astonishment. That anyone should *demand* to see him. Or that his well-trained staff should not be able to escort a lone female off his premises, no matter how *demanding* she was. Either eventuality was extraordinary.

His curiosity grew. 'Who is she?'

'She refuses to give her name, *kyrie.*'

Stavros raised an eyebrow. 'And yet her presence here bothers you? She isn't Press?' Intriguing.

'She says not. No Press card. Not the right attitude either.'

Stavros forbore to query that. His staff were professionals, they knew their business.

'And...?' Of course there was more.

'And she says it's urgent she sees you, speaks with you privately.'

If he made time for every crank, competitor or journalist who wanted to see him, Stavros would never have privacy. Or time to run the most exclusive fine jewellery enterprise in the world.

The House of Denakis had a generations' old reputation for magnificent artistic creations, avidly acquired by the wealthiest of the international élite. Its pieces were worn by royalty, if they could afford it. It set the standard to which other houses aspired. Managing it required not only dedication, flair and outstanding business acumen, but also ruthless single-mindedness.

He curbed his impatience as Petros pulled out a palmsized portable monitor and handed it over. The screen showed a young woman sitting on a straight-backed chair in a bare room. Her back was to the camera but Stavros could see she wore the ubiquitous modern uniform of jeans and a T-shirt. She was slim. Dark hair pinned up on the back of her head.

Her posture caught his attention. She sat straight and alert in her hard seat. But it wasn't nerves that made her sit so. She didn't project an aura of apprehension. Instead her bearing seemed almost regal.

He frowned at her air of confidence. Who was she to be so sure of herself after trespassing onto his property? For a moment something about her nagged at his subconscious. Could he know her? Have met her perhaps?

He shrugged. It didn't matter. She hadn't been invited so he didn't intend to see her.

'Show her off the premises,' he said as he passed the monitor back. 'She's wasting your time.'

But still Petros lingered. He cleared his throat.

Stavros tilted one impatient eyebrow.

'There's more, *kyrie.* You may wish to consider meeting her.'

'And why would I do that?'

There was no doubting Petros' discomfort now.

'She has your ring. With your family seal.'

Stavros froze. He stared into his security chief's hard features. This wasn't a con. The ring was distinctive, one of a kind, and Petros had been with the family long enough to know the genuine item when he saw it.

Even though the ring had been missing now for four years.

'You have it?' Stavros held out his hand, but Petros shook his head.

'I've seen it, examined it closely. But she has it on a long chain round her neck and refuses to give it up till she sees you. I could have taken it from her but it seemed best to wait and be sure…'

To be sure just who this woman was.

Again Stavros experienced that jab of curiosity. Its intensity disturbed him.

There were no unwelcome surprises in his life. He paid an army of staff very well to ensure just that. Even his professional life followed the anticipated pattern—the pattern he laid out for it. There were challenges, goals and opportunities but, with his formidable business skills, his extreme wealth and above all his determination, success was guaranteed.

His ring.

He took a slow breath as he registered the turmoil of almost-buried emotions.

It was his duty to get the piece back if he could, to pass on to the next generation. It had been ancient when one of his ancestors had worn it into battle during the War of Independence. Old even when an earlier ancestor had travelled to Byzantium seeking the emperor's favour.

And it held more recent memories too. Of a time he'd rather forget.

Of the only time in his life that he'd failed.

'Come!' He turned his back on the noise of his engagement celebration. 'Show me this woman who claims to have my property.'

Tessa refused to give in to the exhaustion that threatened to swamp her now she'd finally arrived. She pushed her shoulders back, lifted her chin and prepared to wait.

Just a little longer, and then it would be over. Then she could rest.

She surveyed the blank white wall in front of her. The bare table, the empty chair. What was this room used for? It looked like an interrogation cell.

She shivered as a flash of memory burst upon her. Of another small, windowless room. Not so pristine, or so quiet. The paint on those walls had long since peeled away, leaving the slapdash structure of mortar and cheap bricks visible. The floor was gritty underfoot and littered with debris.

And the smell. Her nostrils flared as she remembered.

That room had been rank with the scent of fear. Fear and pain.

Resolutely she turned her mind back to the present. She was half a world away, literally, from that place. And that room no longer existed, had long since been bulldozed into rubble.

The trouble was that memories couldn't be destroyed as easily as buildings.

She took a deep breath and automatically reached for her talisman on its chain. Its weight was comforting between her breasts. It had seen her through hard times, a promise of hope in times of need and despair.

And now she'd come to give it back. She didn't need it any more.

It had been a shock to discover its real owner was very much alive. She must have sat, statue-still, for long minutes as she'd stared at the magazine, right into the face of the man who'd haunted her for the last four years. The airport lounge had receded to a peripheral blur as she took in his unmistakable features. His arrogant air of assured power.

'*The golden couple: Stavros Denakis and Angela Christophorou. Will it be wedding rings for two?*' So the caption had run.

The photo above it had shown a glamorous couple entering a nightclub. She was gorgeous, model-chic in a figure-moulding silver dress that revealed a fashionable amount of superb cleavage. And an even more stunning amount of diamond jewellery.

Yet she was overshadowed by the presence of the man beside her, tall and powerfully built, his face severe and not a little intimidating as he stared right into the camera. A man with a purpose. With power. With the sort of magnetism a woman couldn't ignore.

Tessa swallowed against the lump of emotion that clogged her throat. She still remembered the surprisingly comforting touch of his hand, enclosing hers. The brush of his lips, fleeting but hot, like a brand against her own. The way his charcoal eyes had darkened almost to black as he'd stared down at her.

Amazing that she could remember such minute detail after all this time, even down to the tremor of excitement that had skittered down her spine at his scrutiny.

But then, he was the man who'd saved her life.

Every minute they'd spent together was emblazoned in

her mind. Through the intervening years she'd revisited that time so often, drawing strength from the recollection of his formidable will-power, his unhesitating, almost casual acceptance of the need to help her.

The memory of the man himself had been a far more potent talisman than the piece of jewellery he'd left behind.

The sound of footsteps, rapid and purposeful, broke across her thoughts and she stiffened in her seat, preparing herself to face him.

The lock clicked and the door swung open and there he was. Stavros Denakis.

Her eyes widened as she took him in. He was bigger than she remembered, so powerfully built across the shoulders that he filled the doorway. She watched his hand clench white-knuckled on the door knob and his chest expand as he drew in a deep breath.

His face might have been sculpted in stone, the flesh tight over a magnificent bone structure. There was a flash of white as his lips drew back for an instant in an expression of shock. His eyes bored into her, dark and doubting. They narrowed as they swept from her head to her waist—all he could see of her behind the table.

Tessa felt that scrutiny like a physical touch and tilted her chin up, her eyes meeting his.

Recognition flared through her. It wasn't just the sight of him but the way she responded to his presence—the quickened pulse, the breathless constriction of her chest, the tell-tale quiver of excitement as she looked up at him.

She'd know this man in the dark, blindfolded.

He'd affected her like that the first time they'd met. Why should she be surprised to discover that hadn't changed?

He strode forward and came to a halt just in front of the small table.

'Who are you?' he demanded in English. His voice was

deep, a mere whisper, but with the sort of authority that guaranteed an answer.

'Tessa Marlowe.' She swallowed against the sudden dryness in her mouth.

He jerked his head up abruptly in clear rejection. For a moment there was silence between them, broken only by the sound of her shallow breathing. Then he leaned forward, planting both fists on the table before her. His head loomed close to hers and she stiffened against the urge to retreat, shrink back in her chair.

She breathed deep, searching for calm. But instead another sensation ricocheted through her. The subtle, tantalising scent of him evoked something unmistakable, a female awareness that circled and curled in on itself, deep in the pit of her belly.

'Don't you remember me?' she whispered, her voice hoarse with stress.

His eyes looked obsidian-black now, slitted and gleaming between long lashes.

There was no recognition there. No welcome. Only doubt. And fury.

'Who are you?' he said again.

'I told you. I'm Tessa Marlowe.'

He slammed his palm against the table. 'No! Tessa Marlowe died four years ago.'

The air seemed to crackle, the tension between them sucking the oxygen from her lungs.

She'd expected surprise, astonishment, but not this anger that welled from him in waves. The force of it pinned her against the hard back of her seat.

She gathered her strength and spoke, surprised to hear her voice so calm and cool. 'You're mistaken. I was injured, unconscious. But that's all.'

He gazed at her, unblinking. 'Prove it.'

She fumbled at the neckline of her T-shirt. Drew the familiar chain up till she felt it in her hand: the ring she'd protected and cherished all these years.

For a moment she hesitated, held it close in her clenched fist. Then she dragged it out, holding the chain at full length away from her, its burden resting in her open palm.

He watched her intently, didn't even blink. A sizzle of energy jagged between them and she wondered why she hadn't heard the sound of a thunderclap to accompany it.

Then he flicked his eyes from hers and down to the prize she held in her hand.

Released from his thrall, she sagged in her seat, exhausted by the assault this man made on her senses.

She heard the hiss of his indrawn breath and knew that at last he believed.

Stavros stared, unbelieving, at the ring in the centre of her slender palm.

He'd recognise it anywhere, had known it all his life. The heavy circlet of gold, worn but still solid. Its centrepiece engraved in ancient times with tiny, exquisite carvings of a hunter in a chariot facing a lion at bay. It had been designed for use untold generations ago as a seal—the unique identifying mark of a man of power.

And now it was the symbol of his house, the House of Denakis. A stylised version of that chariot, that hunter, graced the doors of Denakis showrooms in Athens, Paris, London, New York, Zurich and Tokyo.

He reached out a hand and touched the engraved surface of it. His finger connected with the warmth of her palm and he watched her tremble.

So, she was nervous after all. With her uptilted chin and her unwavering gaze she gave the appearance of pure confidence.

He focused again on the ring. No doubt about it: it was

genuine, and completely out of place on that cheap, low-grade chain.

He frowned. Explanations were required.

Stavros picked up the ring between his fingers, again letting his fingers brush the flesh of her palm. This time she whipped her hand away, leaving him in sole possession of the ring.

He pretended to study it, but his attention was focused on *her*. The rapid rise and fall of her breasts. The soft sound of her breathing. The warm, soap scent of her, more evocative somehow than the expensive designer perfumes to which he was accustomed.

He let the ring drop, watched the shabby chain fall against her plain T-shirt, between her breasts. Then he raised his eyes again to hers.

Even now, prepared for it, he was stunned by the sight of her. When he'd entered the room he'd thought he'd seen a ghost. Reaction had stopped him in his tracks, churning his stomach.

Tessa Marlowe had died four years ago in an explosion that claimed a dozen lives. He had a copy of her death certificate! Officially she didn't exist any more. The memory of the day she'd died, of mangled vehicles in that shambles of a street, lived with him still.

And yet, here she was. *Alive*. The shock of it reverberated down his spine.

Fleetingly he wondered what poor nameless woman had been wrongly identified after the bomb blast. For he knew with a bone-deep certainty that *this* was Tessa Marlowe. The high, slanted cheekbones, the elegant neck and heart-shaped face. The slight frame. And of course those eyes.

He'd seen green eyes before, but not this pure, unadulterated emerald. He'd only found that shade in the most priceless gems. Collectors would pay a fortune for a stone that colour. It was unique.

This was indeed Tessa Marlowe. She was unmistakable.

Yet she looked different. There was a gravity about her, and something in those bright eyes that hinted she'd seen far more of life than she wanted to. Physically she'd altered as well. She'd been slim the first time he'd seen her. Now she seemed fragile. Yet her lips were soft and well-shaped, an invitation in that lovely face.

Oh, yes, he remembered that mouth. Had dreamed of it for months after their meeting.

'What are you doing here?' It emerged from his throat as a growl.

He saw her eyes widen.

What? She thought he'd welcome her after all this time? Accept her presence with no questions or recriminations?

She couldn't be that naïve. Anyone who tried to make trouble for him lived to regret it.

'I came to return it. The ring.' As she spoke she reached for the catch on the chain and opened it. It took an inordinate amount of time for her to slide the ring off and hold it out to him.

Her hand was shaking when she did so.

'And why are you bringing it back to me now? What possible explanation could you have?'

Her brows drew together in a good imitation of confusion. 'It's yours. I know you didn't intend for me to have it this long. If I'd been able to return it earlier, I would have.' She thrust her hand out, closer to him.

On a surge of angry energy he reached out and clasped her whole hand in his, curving his fingers right round hers, pressing the heavy ring into her flesh, into his.

'I'm to believe that it took you this long to contact me? Four whole years?' His tone was rough, furious, and he felt its effect as her hand quivered in his.

He felt no remorse. This woman deserved no sympathy. She'd deceived him for years.

He refused to acknowledge the temptation she represented as he held her warm, soft flesh against his. His body might respond to her. But he had mastery over such basic instincts.

Whatever her game she'd more than met her match with Stavros Denakis.

'I don't believe it,' he said with heavy emphasis, ignoring the flare of what looked like pain in her eyes. This woman was no innocent, he reminded himself. She was out for all she could get. She'd just found a more intriguing way than most to try cashing in.

'But it's true,' she answered. 'I found out about you and I had to come.'

Of course she did. She'd found out precisely who he was and immediately come running. Almost unbelievable that she hadn't worked it out before. But he could understand her decision to locate him once she knew his identity. And the size of his personal fortune.

Her lower lip trembled for an instant, then stilled. She straightened her shoulders and stared straight back at him, the picture of unblemished innocence.

'I'm sorry if I've come at a bad time. It wasn't my intention.' She tugged at her hand but he kept it in his. 'I'll leave now that you have your property.'

Would she indeed? And no doubt she'd head to the nearest Press agency to sell her story.

Not if he had anything to do with it!

'I'm afraid not,' he murmured.

'But I'm not welcome here. That much is obvious.'

He nodded, acknowledging her point. 'True. But do you really think I'm so stupid as to leave you to your own devices?'

She opened her mouth, no doubt to protest. He cut her off with a single, abrupt gesture.

'Enough! I want no more of your pretensions to inno-cence. You will not leave the estate until I have the whole story from you and we come to some…accommodation about our circumstances.'

'Accommodation?' She shook her head, the very picture of bewilderment.

Her dramatic skills had improved in the last four years, he realised. When they'd first met he'd found her amazingly transparent in her thoughts and emotions. Now look at her: an accomplished liar.

'Of course, an accommodation. The situation requires careful…attention.' His fingers tightened round hers as he smiled.

'You surely don't think I'd have celebrated my betrothal quite so publicly tonight if I'd known I still had a wife?'

CHAPTER TWO

TESSA'S lungs emptied on a whoosh of air as she stared up at him, towering over her. She'd known his engagement was a possibility yet still his announcement shocked her, leaving an inexplicable hollow feeling in the pit of her stomach.

Her reaction was nonsensical. He didn't have a role in her life. His relationships were no business of hers.

And yet he'd called her his wife.

The idea was preposterous. They both knew the truth: she'd never been that.

Tessa flinched at the travesty of a smile he turned on her. It was feral. His expression had a definite predatory edge that made her wish she were anywhere but here.

She could almost imagine him sinking those strong white teeth into the soft skin at the base of her neck. Either that or wrapping his hands around her there to squeeze the breath out of her.

She looked into his face and for a moment knew fear.

Then logic asserted itself. He might be furious, might even want to hurt her, but Stavros Denakis was a civilised man. His previous actions had surely proved that.

She wondered if he had any idea how tightly he grasped her hand.

'You're hurting me,' she said quietly, staring back into his blazing eyes.

He blinked and released her. Instantly blood throbbed back into her hand and she winced.

There was a thud as the heavy ring dropped and she looked down to see it spinning on the table between them. Above it was her outstretched palm, dwarfed by his. Both bore the deep imprint of the ring. Her hand was trembling and she drew it sharply back into her lap, massaging it against the pins and needles that prickled there.

'My apologies,' he said in a toneless voice.

But her mind was already racing, processing the information he'd flung at her in such lashing anger.

'You're going to be married?'

'Amusing, isn't it?' Yet there was no humour in that flash of a smile he turned on her. 'I find myself in the unlikely position of possessing both a wife and a fiancée.'

She squeezed her eyes shut for a moment against a sudden swirl of dizziness. What on earth was he talking about? None of this made sense. Not to a brain numbed by shock and far too many wakeful hours.

'I…don't know what to say.'

'Don't you?' His deep voice was taunting. 'You surprise me. I thought you'd have it all worked out. Have you decided on a dollar amount? Or is it euros you prefer?'

'Euros? I don't understand what you're talking about.' She shook her head and the room spun, the edges of her vision blurring, making her glad she was sitting.

There was definite meaning behind his words. An accusation even. But her mind was too foggy to process it.

She should have stopped to rest in Athens before coming on to find him. Should have taken the time to sleep and eat and recuperate. From South America to the United States—an internal flight there and a lengthy delay due to some engine problem—then the leg to Greece, the chaos of Athens and finding her way by public transport to the port of Piraeus; finally the ferry to this island in the Saronic Gulf… Tessa's journey had taken forever.

She was exhausted. The shock of discovering him to be alive and the strain of uncertainty had kept her too keyed-up to sleep even through the tedium of flights and airport delays. Now the long hours without rest took their toll.

She grasped the edge of the table with both hands and clung on tight. With an effort she forced back the strange, woozy feeling and stiffened her spine.

Tessa wasn't up to facing this angry stranger. He wasn't at all like her recollection of him. Had her treasured memories been a case of rose-tinted glasses?

Perhaps she should have heeded the cowardly inner voice that had urged her to forget what had happened and scurry home to Australia. To leave the past safely buried.

'Enough!' His hand thumped, palm down, onto the table and she jumped, eyes widening. 'I don't have time for these games. It's obvious why you're here. There's no point prevaricating.'

His dark eyes probed as he thrust his head close to hers across the table. Animosity vibrated from him in waves, a palpable force. He was trying to intimidate her into submission.

And he was doing an excellent job!

Tessa shoved her chair back and got to her feet, thankful for the support of the table. Her knees were absurdly wobbly.

'Where do you think you're going? You're not leaving until I'm finished with you.'

And when would that be? His fury seemed infinite.

'I'm just putting myself on a more equal footing,' she replied quietly. She'd learned through bitter experience that a calm demeanour was the safest response to hostility.

His glare didn't diminish but he stood back a fraction from

the table. Even that small distance seemed to lessen the impact of his sparking hostility and she breathed more easily.

'So how much do you want?' he demanded.

'How much what?'

'*Sto Diavolo!*' He rolled his eyes towards the ceiling. 'I have no patience for this game of yours. Can't you manage a direct answer to a simple question?'

'I would if I knew what the question was.' She raised her palm when he would have spoken. 'But perhaps it will ease your mind if I tell you I didn't come here to get anything from you. I only came to return the ring.'

She looked down at the table and the familiar ornament lying on the wood. She blinked. Stupid to feel sentimental about a chunk of jewellery. She didn't need a good-luck charm any more.

She raised her eyes to his and strove to ignore the sizzle of heat that blasted out at her.

'There's one more thing,' she said, shuffling her feet as a wave of tiredness made her unsteady.

'Of course there is. At last we come to it.' There was contempt on his face and a sneer curved his sensual mouth as he crossed his arms over his chest. The action emphasised the power of his body, even in a superbly tailored evening jacket. He radiated sheer masculine force.

She shook her head and then wished she hadn't, when it took a moment to bring him back into focus.

'I came to thank you,' she said and held out her hand to him.

That took him aback. He stared at her as if he'd never shaken hands before.

'If it hadn't been for you,' she continued, 'I'd be dead. You saved my life.' Her lips curved in a tentative smile. 'I never got to thank you for that, but I wanted you to know that I didn't forget. I owe you so much.'

'What nonsense is this?' His brows furrowed heavily and he ignored her gesture. His face grew dark with anger.

Disappointed, Tessa let her arm drop, her stamina seeping away at his abrupt rejection. The nervous energy that had kept her on the move for days bled away in a sudden rush, leaving her weightless and hollow.

She ought to sit, regroup and gather her strength. But his eyes held her spellbound.

'You have the temerity to come here and spin me such a tale? Do you take me for a fool?' He stood up straighter, stretching to his full, formidable height. 'I'm afraid for your sake I'm not that gullible. It takes more than a pretty face to convince me.'

The muscles in Tessa's abdomen tightened convulsively as if absorbing a physical blow—such was the repressed violence in him. She set her jaw and ignored the sudden glaze of heat behind her eyes.

'In that case there's no more to be said.' Tessa dragged her gaze from his. So he didn't accept her gratitude. That was his problem, not hers.

What sort of man could be so lacking in charity or trust or even common courtesy?

'I'll be on my way, then.' His face was a blur as she turned quickly to her backpack, propped against the wall. Giddiness rocked her as he stepped close, hemming her in.

'I *said,* you won't leave until we sort this out.' He glared down at her, nostrils flared and jaw clenched, the epitome of male displeasure.

'And *I've* said all I intend to say.' Tessa snapped her teeth shut against the temptation to call him a bullying lout. 'As far as I'm concerned we've covered everything. You've got your ring and it's time for me to leave.'

'Straight into the waiting arms of the paparazzi? I think not.'

The Press? What would she want with the Press? Tessa had

other concerns right now, like where she'd find a bed for the night. She hoped she had enough cash to tide her over. She hadn't counted on a side-trip to Greece when she'd begun her journey in South America.

It had been a stupid impulse after all.

'I have no intention of talking to any paparazzi,' she assured him. 'So you can stop your fuming and step out of my way.'

Slowly he shook his head and she read the speculation in his dark grey eyes. Speculation and something else she couldn't put a name to. But it made the hairs rise on the back of her neck.

'You have no right to keep me here.' Despite her rising anxiety Tessa's voice sounded oddly muted, as if it came from a long distance away.

His lips curved up in a sinister smile that sent a shudder rippling down her backbone.

'What about the right of a husband?' he murmured. 'A husband long-deprived of his lovely wife.'

He stepped close, bringing his powerful body flush against hers. His heat radiated into her, searing her through her shabby clothes. But it was the menace in his expression that sucked the breath from her.

'You'll find that here in Greece we take the responsibilities, and the *rights* of a husband very seriously.'

Something sizzled in his eyes, molten hot and arresting. She felt her reaction to it, a feverish trembling, right through her body. That frightened her more than anything else.

'Then I hope your fiancée knows exactly what she's getting herself into.' Tessa angled her chin up and met his eyes, glare for glare. But she had no hope of outfacing him. This man had all the self-confidence of a deity.

'Enough! This is getting us nowhere.'

'I couldn't agree more.' She sidestepped him and took a single pace towards her luggage. Then two things happened simultaneously: a large hand manacled her elbow and her shaky legs crumpled beneath her.

She heard a rush of incomprehensible invective as the room tilted wildly and his dark eyes—large and disbelieving—swam before her.

She stiffened her knees, bracing herself against the dizziness. But already he was bending, scooping her up in his arms and tucking her tight against his deep chest.

He encompassed her. Those strong arms curved underneath, supporting her. His powerful chest cushioned her. And his eyes…his eyes meshed with hers, lustrous and compelling. She felt as if they looked into her very soul. Everything about him radiated male dominance: from the bunched muscles binding her close to the arrogant jut of his nose. Even the hint of dark shadow on his hard jaw reinforced the impression of primal *machismo*.

And something else, something unsettling eddied around her, drawing her nerves to attention. It was the scent of his skin, she realised as she gazed at his mask-still features. Like tangy pine and earthy male. Intriguing. Inviting. Tempting.

Blood pulsed loud in her ears as she stared at him. Her heart throbbed heavily, echoing the steady beat she felt deep inside his chest. Her mouth dried as the world shrank to just the two of them. Close, closer…

'There's no need for this,' she whispered, surprised to find her voice so reedy. 'I can stand.'

She might not have spoken.

'What have you been doing, starving yourself?' One large hand splayed across her ribcage, right under her breast. His fingers slid experimentally across her ribs and back again, almost as if he were counting them. He scowled, his brows tilting at a ferocious angle.

'When did you last eat?'

'I had something on the plane.' A cup of coffee and dry

crackers somewhere over the Atlantic. Flying still made her nervous and that was all she'd been able to stomach.

She looked into his dark gold face, into his gleaming, furious eyes, and felt a tightening in her chest, as if someone had squeezed her heart.

'*Christos!* What did you intend to do? Make a grand entrance and then collapse at my feet in a bid for sympathy?'

Tessa wriggled in his arms, trying to loosen his hold so she could stand on her own feet. But his grip remained firm and unforgiving.

Anger surged through her. He had no cause to treat her like this. She'd only been trying to do the right thing, and she'd come all this way!

So much for the famed Greek hospitality she'd heard about.

'I have no interest in your sympathy, *Mr* Denakis.' She spat out the words, tasting bitter disillusionment on her tongue. 'I don't know what your problem is. We don't *have* a relationship. We never did. And,' she cut across him as he opened his mouth to speak, 'I'm not interested in meeting any journalists.' She swallowed, trying to moisten her parched mouth. Her sudden burst of energy was fading fast. 'Now I'd appreciate it if you'd put me down.'

For a moment she saw a hint of puzzlement in his eyes. Then the impression was gone, ousted by the sheer arrogance of his flared nostrils and raised brows as he looked down his impressive, aristocratic nose at her.

'A fine performance, madam. Truly masterful. But you and I both know it was just that: a performance. We're bound to each other, until such time as I decide how best to sever the connection.'

He swung round towards the door so quickly that the room blurred around her.

'We will discuss this somewhere more congenial. I, for one, have no desire to continue this discussion here.'

He looked away and she was left gazing up at the underside of his sharply angled jaw, the plane of his cheek and his well-shaped ear.

It was like looking at the man she remembered, but through a distorting glaze of anger. Briefly she wondered if Stavros Denakis had an evil twin. Or whether the man she'd met four years ago had been an impostor.

But it was the same man. There could be no mistaking the way her heart accelerated just being close to him, or the hint of longing that tinged her anger.

It was appalling but true: Tessa had never reacted to anyone else this way. Now she discovered that the only man to make her feel so *aware* was an egotistical, bad-tempered brute!

It was typical of her luck.

'You find this situation humorous?' His deep voice rumbled up from his chest, a vibration she felt as well as heard. 'Believe me, you won't find it funny by the time I've finished with you.'

'No!' Tessa gritted her teeth while she searched for a calm tone. 'I don't find it at all amusing to be manhandled.'

He stopped in mid-stride and stared down at her. An overhead light haloed his hair, turning him into a dark vengeful angel. His eyes were impenetrable.

'Is that a threat?' he asked softly. 'A hint of harassment litigation to come?'

The suppressed violence in his tone made her shiver. She clenched her hands against the impulse to do something stupid such as try to claw her way out of his unforgiving grip. She knew instinctively that he'd have no compunction about using his superior strength to stop her.

'I have no interest in a lawsuit. *But* that doesn't mean you can ride roughshod over me.' She snatched a quick breath before her courage faded. 'Now, I'd be grateful if you'd put me down. I prefer to walk.'

For a long moment he scrutinised her with all the hauteur of a prince surveying some upstart lackey. Tessa felt the blood warm her cheeks, so intense was that survey. And so disapproving.

Then his mouth tilted up at one side in a self-satisfied smirk that disappeared almost before she registered it.

'You'll find it easier to do things the way *I* wish them to be done.'

And then he was stalking down the long corridor again, holding her effortlessly, ignoring everything she'd said.

They passed a series of closed doors and then he swung round a corner, exiting the building under a covered walkway. The soft, balmy night air caressed her skin and she breathed deeply, trying to calm her racing pulse. From somewhere nearby came the sound of people, lots of people, enjoying themselves. Through the jumble of voices she heard a thread of music.

A party. She'd arrived when he was entertaining, and by the sound of it this was no intimate family gathering. That might explain the tension in him when he'd stormed in to confront her.

But nothing could excuse his behaviour since.

Tessa blinked back hot, futile tears at the realisation that the man she'd put on a pedestal for all these years was the sort of arrogant bully she most detested.

How had she got it so wrong?

And why did it matter? After tonight they'd never see each other again.

The walkway ended at another, larger building. He barely slowed his pace to negotiate the door and another corridor. There was no similarity between this architect-designed palace and the utilitarian security block they'd just left. The rooms here were discreetly opulent. Fresh flowers scented the air and there were fine furnishings, artfully placed, designed for both comfort and display. Spacious. Luxurious. The home of a mega-wealthy man.

The magazine had been right after all: Stavros Denakis had more money than she'd ever dreamed of. The divide between them was impossible to breach.

The realisation chilled her and she slumped in his hold.

She'd known from the first that he wasn't like other men. His absolute self-assurance, his willingness to take charge, his split-second decision-making, even in traumatic circumstances, the power and confidence he radiated... She'd been so grateful for those qualities the day he'd rescued her. But now at last she understood—they were simply the qualities of a man used to command, a man with the riches to buy whatever he wanted.

The knowledge destroyed the last shred of her treasured dreams—the secret romantic image of the man who'd snatched her from the threat of torture and death.

Through four arduous years of hardship she'd fantasised that one day a man like him, a man with those same qualities, might find her. And when they met he wouldn't act out of necessity, but out of desire. For her.

That old impossible longing to be loved just for herself. It was a wonder she hadn't grown out of it after all she'd been through.

Stavros strode into the sitting room of a guest suite. The one nearest to his own rooms. He'd keep this troublemaker under close scrutiny until he sorted out a solution to the diabolical mess she'd created.

She lay passive in his arms now, as limp as a doll. No more of those useless struggles.

He'd been relieved to feel her surge of energy as she tried to escape his hold. She looked so fragile, her eyes huge in her delicately moulded face, her body more than slim. But she was surprisingly strong. Not enough to push him away, of course, but enough to reassure him that she wasn't at death's door.

That would be an unnecessary complication.

The situation was already fraught enough. The sizzle of connection he felt whenever he met Tessa Marlowe's green-eyed gaze warned him of added danger. A flicker of heat burned his skin as he inhaled her fresh soap scent. It blazed when he thought about the way her body fitted perfectly in his arms. And it had nothing to do with his righteous fury. It hinted at something much more basic.

Yet he refused to acknowledge any attraction to this cheap, unprincipled opportunist.

The sharp possessive pleasure he experienced, clasping her tight to his chest, feeling her soft hair tease his neck, was an illusion. The product of shock at seeing her again. It couldn't be anything else.

Nevertheless, the sooner he put some distance between them, the better. For even in her underfed state, Tessa Marlowe had curves in all the right places. Curves that his hands itched to explore.

He lowered her onto a nearby sofa, his movements abrupt. Immediately he straightened and stepped back, furious at the way her scent lingered in his nostrils, feeding the edgy awareness deep inside him. His temperature had climbed a couple of degrees too, a reaction to holding her feminine form so intimately close.

Damnation!

He turned away, picked up the internal phone and snapped out an order for coffee, food and ouzo.

This would take time to sort out. Time he didn't have. Damn it all, he had his engagement party to attend!

A hot tide of fury roared through him.

How *dared* she put him in this position?

He swung round to confront her, his lips already forming a stinging rebuke. But the words jammed in his throat.

She was silently weeping, her face angled away from him and her head pressed back against the cushioned seat. There were no tears on her cheeks, but her eyes brimmed with them, glittering crystalline-bright in the lamp-light.

She looked distraught.

Guilt rippled through him but he crushed it instantly.

She was simply a superlative actress, playing the sympathy card. His mind knew it. Even so, the ploy worked.

Unwillingly he recalled the first time he'd seen her. The echo of gunfire in the distance had been a stark contrast to the waiting silence of the tiny, evil-smelling cell. Fear had hung in the air, and despair. She'd had tears in her eyes then too, but she'd blinked them away and scrambled to her feet, adopting a defensive stance that told him all he needed to know about the way she'd been treated.

She'd been desperate, expecting the worst, but ready to fight.

And he'd responded immediately. Not only to the need to rescue her from a dire situation, but more: to her gorgeous face, her tempting body.

No! He refused to go there.

Whatever had happened four years ago, he knew exactly why she was here now. To milk him for all she could get.

He was no gullible fool, to be sucked in by a show of female emotion. She'd underestimated him if she thought he'd dance to her tune just because she shed a few tears.

'I'm listening,' he growled, planting his fists on his hips and ignoring the way she flinched at his threatening tone. 'What is your asking price?'

Tessa blinked back the burning film of tears, berating herself for getting so emotional. The last thing she wanted was to display weakness before this man.

His temper vibrated, almost out of control, between them.

'There is no price.' She looked across the room at a bright abstract painting, avoiding his hard stare.

'My patience is at an end,' he barked. 'You will get no more by delaying. In fact, for every minute you keep me waiting, the final settlement will be cut.'

Tessa frowned. 'I don't understand.'

A flurry of outraged Greek singed her ears and in the next instant a large body invaded her space, crowding her back against the corner of the sofa.

Large hands grabbed hers, yanking her around so that she faced him as he sat beside her. Searing heat surged into her, from his touch, his body, his glittering eyes.

He was furious, grim, dangerous.

And he was the sexiest man she'd ever seen.

Her throat closed in panic.

'Tell me now,' he whispered, and the softly menacing tone scared her more than his earlier outrage. 'Exactly how much will it cost me to be free of you?'

'I... Nothing,' she croaked, wondering suddenly if he meant to harm her.

His hands tightened round her wrists. His jaw clenched in a spasm of tension. His eyes burned into hers.

'I will be free of you, either by annulment or divorce, whatever is faster. And I will pay a reasonable amount to purchase your silence, with a watertight, legally binding agreement.'

Tessa's eyes widened as she watched his lips move, heard his words. Yet they didn't make sense. This was crazy!

'But there's no need. We were never married!'

'*Sto Diavolo!* Of course we were married. Why else would you have my ring? Why else would you be here, angling for my money?'

She shook her head and the room swirled round her. She was almost glad of his tight grip holding her steady.

'But the man who performed the ceremony—he wasn't a priest. The ceremony was a sham, a ploy to help me escape.'

His eyes bored into hers and something twisted in the pit

of her stomach. For an instant she thought she saw a flicker of doubt in his expression.

But then he was speaking again, slowly, clearly, almost brutally. She fought to catch her breath as his words pounded into her brain.

'He wasn't a priest. He was from the local town hall and he was legally empowered to marry us.' His words were slow, deliberate and unavoidable. 'Everything was done legally, even the witnesses for the official record.'

Tessa opened her mouth to gasp in some oxygen, to protest. But his words continued: remorseless, fantastic.

'The marriage was legitimate,' said Stavros Denakis. There was a bitter twist to his lips, utter distaste in his eyes.

'We are husband and wife.'

CHAPTER THREE

TESSA's pulse galloped, loud in the raw silence that echoed with his words. Her hollow stomach cramped.

'You're not joking, are you?' she whispered at last when she found her voice.

The mocking slant of his eyebrows betrayed scorn. That expression of disdain on his hard, aristocratic face made him look like some superior pagan god.

'I do not joke about such things.' He leaned back against the leather sofa and crossed his arms over his deep chest. Scepticism and impatience radiated from him.

And still she felt the sizzle of heat where his hands had encircled her skin.

'Are you sure?' she was desperate enough to ask. 'Absolutely sure?' That day had been so chaotic after all.

'Your show of astonishment is truly touching,' he murmured. 'But don't keep up the act on my account.'

She winced as his sarcasm flayed her fragile self-possession. The man's tongue was pure poison.

'You really believe I would make a mistake about something like that?' He paused, his eyes narrowing as he scanned her features. 'I even have the wedding certificate to prove it. Signed, witnessed and legally binding.'

Tessa sank back into the embrace of soft leather, her mind racing.

She was married? Had been married for four years?

She pressed a hand to her chest where a sharp knot of shock bruised her. She was married to *him?*

'But why did you use a justice of the peace? It didn't have to be a *real* marriage. Just something to…'

'To get you out of prison?' No mistaking the sneer in his tone. It matched his frosty eyes and the curl of his lip. His expression was judgemental, dismissive.

'Any stranger would have done.' Tessa refused to be cowed. If this was true, this ridiculous situation was *his* fault, not hers! 'There was no need actually to *marry* me!'

'Believe me,' he leaned close and the wrath simmering in his eyes forced her back away from him, 'if there'd been an alternative, any alternative, I would have taken it.'

His gaze held her in a grip so powerful she could barely breathe. She felt as if her ribs were in a vice, constricting the flow of air to her lungs.

'It may have escaped your notice,' he said, 'but a little town the size of San Miguel can be remarkably short of helpful strangers willing to perjure themselves in order to rescue a foreigner from the local gaol.

'Time was short and I'd already had enough trouble persuading your gaolers to let me see you, let alone permit a wedding on the premises.'

Her head swam and she shut her eyes. She'd walked into a nightmare. If only she hadn't given in to the compulsion to see him again, the man she'd believed for years had given his life to save hers.

'It was a real marriage or nothing,' he continued, his voice like rough velvet against her abraded nerves. 'As you very well knew.'

Her eyes snapped open. They were back to that again. He

was a man of such persistent suspicion. For a fleeting moment Tessa wondered what had made him so distrustful.

'I knew *none* of this. Nothing at all until just now.'

She watched the shimmer of disbelief glaze his eyes and his jaw harden impatiently. There was no way she'd ever convince him. He was determined to believe she'd somehow deliberately trapped him into marriage.

If the idea weren't so fantastic, and so appalling, she'd be laughing her head off. *Her* snaring some uppity billionaire with an ego the size of South America! As if!

'Why didn't you *say* something at the time?'

'What?' He shook his head. 'You wished me to apologise within earshot of the celebrant and the prison guards that our hasty plans had changed? That we'd have to make do with a real wedding and worry about dissolving the marriage later? You really think they'd have let us proceed?' His dark brows arched in mock-surprise.

She squeezed her eyes shut against the spinning sensation that accelerated when she met his glare. If she could just sit here alone. Get her breath. In time she'd work something out. She was a survivor. She had years of practice keeping herself alive. A furious Greek tycoon with an ego problem and a marriage certificate were nothing after what she'd been through. Right?

Tessa clenched her fists, trying to dredge up some energy to deal with this situation. But she was exhausted.

'Here, drink this!'

She opened her eyes to find him leaning over her, filling her vision with his wide shoulders and massive chest. His accusing eyes.

A skitter of sensation scudded down her spine. Trepidation? Anger?

Or something else?

'No, thank you. I don't need—' she spluttered as he pressed

a small glass against her lips and a rocket of aniseed fire blasted into her mouth and down her throat.

Her eyes streamed and she gagged.

'And again.' His fingers fastened around her chin, tilting it up towards the glass. His hand was warm and easily encompassed her jaw. Against the tempered strength of his hold she felt appallingly vulnerable. Her pulse raced beneath his touch.

She blinked and met his gaze. It was implacable, as relentless as the large hand holding her steady while he tipped another mouthful of liquid between her lips. Heat scorched all the way down to her belly and she shuddered.

'No more.' Her voice was a hoarse gasp. 'What is that stuff?'

'Ouzo. Fierce but effective. It's an acquired taste.'

Tessa wondered who'd be desperate enough to acquire it. But he was right. She wasn't numb any more. Delicious warmth spread through her veins and her stiff muscles relaxed. A strange lassitude invaded her body.

Abruptly he moved away and she almost sighed in relief. She couldn't think when he loomed like that, vibrating dark impatience and animosity.

'Here.' His voice was rough as he pushed a plate into her hand. It was laden with food. She hadn't even noticed anyone come to the door with a tray.

Could that be caviar on the tiny buttered squares of bread? And there were shrimps, savoury pastries, a whole range of delicacies. She swallowed as her salivary glands kicked into gear.

'Eat.' His tone was brusque as he turned away, his stiff back and rigid shoulders eloquent of dismissal.

'I have things to do, but I'm sure you'll make yourself at home in my absence.' No mistaking his sarcasm. 'Just don't think about leaving this room. There will be a guard stationed right outside.' His voice was silky with threat and she shivered, guessing he'd like nothing more than to 'deal' with her if she disobeyed him. His anger was so fiercely controlled she imagined he'd welcome an excuse to unleash it.

He didn't even glance at her as he left. The door closed with a decisive click and Tessa slumped bonelessly into the sofa cushions.

Where did he think she'd go? Did he think she'd prowl through his home? All she wanted was to collect her pack with her passport and the last of her cash, and leave.

But what was the point? They needed to sort out a way to dissolve the marriage—she and Stavros Denakis.

Her mind shied away blindly from the word *husband*.

Tessa stared out of the window to the formal garden, the panorama of dark sea and cloudless sky. Even the air was balmy, scented with salt and the perfume of orange blossom.

It didn't seem right that everything should look so peaceful when she was a mass of jangling nerves, raw from the corrosive memories of last night's confrontation.

Where did that man get off, treating her as though everything were her fault? As if she'd connived to put in him an embarrassing predicament when all she'd wanted was to do the right thing?

She squeezed her eyes shut, appalled at her naïvety. At her spur-of-the-moment impulse, cashing in her airline ticket to Sydney and instead travelling to Greece. As if high-and-mighty Stavros Denakis would be interested in her gratitude after all this time.

She drew in a shuddering breath and blinked to clear her blurred vision, appalled at how near to crying she was. Last night, for the first time in years, hot tears had threatened to fall. Now they stung her eyes again. This weakness after all she'd been through was inexplicable.

Today her actions seemed nothing short of foolish. So what if it had seemed like a sign, like fate, when she'd opened that discarded magazine in the airport lounge and stared straight into the eyes of the man who'd haunted her for four years? The man who'd been at the centre of her secret hopes and dreams as she'd struggled daily against privation and poverty and the temptation to give up hope.

She was no innocent kid. You'd think years of hardship would have taught her there was no point in spinning foolish dreams. Except she hadn't been able to deny those secret fantasies of *him*. Those unsettling night-time imaginings that had been her only solace. Dreams of strong arms, of a determined, powerful saviour coming to her aid. Dreams that had left her edgy and burning with a heat that belied the chilly mountain nights.

Tessa clenched her jaw and straightened. No way would the *real* Stavros Denakis protect her ever again. Not after his fury last night. He must be deeply in love with his fiancée, and enormously protective of her, to view Tessa as any sort of threat.

She breathed deeply, sloughing off a sneaking twinge of self-pity. That would get her nowhere.

She'd spent the morning in a deep, exhausted sleep, waking to a visit from a doctor, organised by her host. As if Stavros Denakis actually cared how she was! He was probably just checking she hadn't brought some highly contagious disease with her from South America.

Her first instinct had been to refuse to be examined, but the doctor had been persuasive and Tessa just anxious enough about her strangely emotional state to comply. It was a relief to have her fears allayed. She was fine. All she needed was time to recover her strength.

But now it was late afternoon and she'd achieved nothing. She'd better contact the Australian embassy in Athens. They'd help her with the legalities and her return to Sydney. Not that there was anything waiting for her there. But she'd be home, where she'd longed to be for years. She'd have access to her bank account, could start rebuilding her life while the lawyers sorted out a divorce.

Tessa swung round from the window to look for a phone, wondering how difficult it would be to place a call to the embassy when she spoke no Greek.

She stopped dead when she met Stavros Denakis' storm-grey eyes.

Her lungs seized up as she met his probing gaze, then she lifted her chin and drew in a slow breath, refusing to be daunted by the sight of him.

He stood just inside the room, his shoulders almost as broad as the closed door behind him. She blinked, realising he'd entered without a sound. A shiver of trepidation trickled down her backbone at the knowledge he must have the sound-less tread of a predator. Like a jungle jaguar.

It made her feel vulnerable. But she shoved her hands into the pockets of her baggy trousers, resisting the impulse to curve her arms defensively around herself.

His expression was shuttered, totally unreadable. Some-how that was more worrying than the blaze of wrath he'd directed at her last night. Fury and bullying she could stand up to. But what was going on in his mind now?

She wasn't foolish enough to believe he'd seen the error of his ways and accepted the truth about her intentions. No, there was a waiting stillness about him, as if he were a hunter sizing up his prey, that sent its own wordless message across the humming silence between them.

Yet to her horror, his patent distrust wasn't enough to prevent the spark of excitement that flared into life deep inside her. He did that to her without even trying.

She'd only ever experienced the sensation with *this* man: a thrill, a yearning that made her seem a stranger to her own body. It scared the hell out of her.

* * *

Stavros watched her eyes widen, the pupils dilating in those green depths, and felt a stab of savage satisfaction. Even from here he sensed her fear, though she stood ramrod-straight, her jaw angled up defiantly.

Good. She deserved to worry about his next move. He'd been tempted to have his staff call the police. They'd keep her locked up while they dealt with the charges. Trespass at least. No doubt they could arrange a few others, perhaps threats of violence or attempted blackmail?

But much as he'd prefer to be rid of her disturbing physical presence, Tessa Marlowe wasn't going anywhere. If he released her into police custody there was a chance her story would leak to the Press. Some tantalising snippet aimed at persuading him to be generous in his settlement.

No. Ms Marlowe would stay right here where he could keep an eye on her.

He rolled his shoulders, still stiff with the strain of repressed anger that had escalated through the night.

Every congratulatory comment at last evening's party, every good wish for a fruitful union, had notched the tension in his gut tighter. For the first time in his life he'd felt a fraud, lying to his family, his friends and to the woman he'd decided to take as his wife.

He didn't like the feeling one iota. Or the sensation of matters being beyond his control. That *he,* who prided himself on his well-regulated world, should be caught in this preposterous situation, barely one step removed from bigamy—it was untenable!

'What do you want?' Her voice was a fraction rough, proof that she wasn't as calm as she tried to appear.

He paced into the room, ignoring the spike of heat in his bloodstream as he approached her. That was the ultimate insult to his pride and his intelligence. The fact that, even recognising her as a greedy opportunist, he wanted her, with a potent longing that astounded him.

Lust had never been so urgently consuming. He had to fight the raw compulsion to reach out and feel her soft flesh beneath his, lose himself in her.

He, a man of honour. Who had just vowed to marry another woman!

No matter that he'd chosen his fiancée because of her impeccable credentials in meeting his requirements for a wife, hostess and mother of his children. No matter that their emotions weren't engaged, or that they'd yet to consummate their relationship. He owed her his loyalty.

He'd spent the night coming to terms with the unpalatable fact that it was Tessa Marlowe who stirred his blood, not his fiancée, Angela. He wouldn't grant this woman the satisfaction of realising it.

'I've come to see if you need anything.'

Her fine brows arched up and the look she sent him could have befitted a supercilious monarch. She really did have attitude.

But they both knew it was a bluff. He had the power to break her if he chose, despite the fact of the marriage contract they'd signed. Money spoke loud and clear. Always. And his sort of wealth could achieve almost anything. She'd do well to remember that.

'What more could I need when my host is so…*generous* with his hospitality?'

Despite himself, Stavros felt his mouth kick up at one corner in appreciation of her reckless courage. Obviously, despite the doctor's concerns, she was fit enough to fight.

He'd come in here expecting to see her languishing at death's door. Severe physical and mental exhaustion, the doctor had said, plus borderline malnutrition and the after-effects of *giardia* from drinking tainted water.

For a while there, Stavros had seriously questioned whether he'd misjudged her. But, seeing her now, it seemed clear the doctor had taken her word about the symptoms and been duped by an excellent actress. As for the malnutrition—starving herself in order to get her hands on several million dollars wasn't out of the question. Unfortunately Stavros had first-hand experience of women unscrupulous enough to do even that. He was long past the age when a sob story and a show of feminine weakness might impress him.

'Don't get too comfortable,' he said abruptly, his deep voice vibrating with disapproval. His straight brows arrowed together and Tessa knew instinctively that he held on to his temper by a thread. 'You'll remain just as long as it takes to devise a solution to this problem.'

'The solution is simple.' She'd worked out that much already. 'All we need to do is annul the marriage. There must be grounds for that.'

He stalked closer and immediately the spacious room shrank around them.

'Non-consummation, perhaps?'

Tessa's whole body thrummed in reaction as she looked up into those watchful grey eyes. They weren't cold any more, she suddenly realised. There was more fire than ice in his expression, and a flash of something that made her insides twist.

Tentatively she slid one foot back a fraction, but there was nowhere to go with the window right behind her. He was still a pace away from her but the intensity of his gaze made her feel cornered and way too vulnerable.

'That's an option.' Tessa had to tilt her face higher to look him in the eye.

'Ah, but that might be difficult to prove. What evidence can we provide?' One sleek, dark eyebrow winged upwards, emphasising his sardonic expression.

'I'm sure the authorities would be willing to accept our word for it. After all, we were only together for a couple of hours—'

'That's not convincing.' Slowly he shook his head but his gaze remained fixed on her, riveting her to the spot. 'A couple of hours are more than enough time to consummate a marriage.' His voice dropped a notch so the words rolled across her flesh like an echo of distant thunder. Tessa shivered as she watched his eyes narrow and his expression change. There was something dangerous about that glint in his eyes. Something feral.

'Or are you, perhaps, doubting my virility?' he added in an undertone.

He didn't move, didn't approach, yet she felt him encroach further into her space. Tessa found her hands splaying wide for support on the window ledge behind her.

'Don't be absurd! I...'

He did crowd her then. With a single long stride he obliterated the distance between them and his heat blazed, raw and unnerving, against her trembling body.

Tessa's nostrils flared in response to the spicy, masculine scent of his skin. Her chest heaved as she sucked in a calming breath and she forced her gaze to flick away from the intimidating wall of his chest, mere centimetres from her breasts. A wave of sensation washed through her, a purely feminine awareness. Her nipples puckered and tightened as if with cold. But she wasn't chilled. Instead her flesh was heating. A wave of fiery warmth spread from her chest up her throat, and Tessa knew that any second now she'd be blushing.

'Or perhaps it's a personal demonstration you're after?' The words contained a sharp, sarcastic sting.

Automatically Tessa shook her head, horrified at how fast the conversation had got out of hand.

'No!' The denial burst from her mouth, strident and appalled.

Reluctantly she focused on his eyes, dark now with unholy anger. Or was it amusement?

She drew in a sharp breath, forcing herself to ignore the graze of her chest against his linen shirt as he leaned closer.

The devil was baiting her! Deliberately toying with her, testing her limits with the unspoken threat of his big body. He wanted her to panic.

'This has gone far enough.' She struggled to sound calm, knowing that was the best way to end this torment. 'I wasn't questioning your masculinity. I was simply observing that the circumstances of our…wedding would support us when we said it was a marriage in name only.'

There, she sounded reasonable. Only a little breathless.

He scrutinised her as if he could read her every secret in her face.

'So you believe the *circumstances* prove we didn't have sex?'

Her eyes widened. 'It was hardly the time or the place. A civil war had just broken out around us!'

'And yet it's a proven fact that in situations of extreme danger, people find comfort in the sexual act. I believe it can be quite a compulsion.'

Had he leaned closer? Or had she swayed towards him? She couldn't be that unsteady on her feet.

'But we didn't even know each other!' Any logical person would see that theirs had been a paper formality, not a real marriage.

'Interesting.' He spoke unhurriedly and she watched his mouth form the word. Despite her uneasiness there was something almost hypnotic about the way those firm lips moved. 'So your contention is that strangers don't have sex? I don't find that particularly convincing. Or are you arguing that *you* would never do such a thing?'

Again, that interrogatory tilt of an eyebrow. It reinforced the imposing, dominant angles of his face, reminding her irresistibly of a fallen angel, beautiful and oh-so-dangerous.

Tessa's hands balled into fists as she repressed the

panicky need to try to force him away from her. She knew it would be futile. He was larger, stronger and far nastier than she was. He'd probably enjoy watching her flail against his superior strength. But she wouldn't give him that cheap satisfaction.

Instead she'd be calm, reasonable, in control. She'd ignore his provocation. No way would she rise to his baiting about her morality.

It was on the tip of her tongue to blurt out that, contrary to his sneering assumption, she *could* provide the evidence to prove their marriage had never been consummated. It was something she'd far rather avoid. It would be a last resort, but if that was what it took to be free of this man then she'd do it.

In the meantime there was no way she'd reveal anything so personal to Stavros Denakis. She didn't even want to think about his derision if he realised her experience was so limited. The mood he was in, he wouldn't believe her.

'My contention,' she responded, looking at a point over his shoulder, 'is that the authorities will have no reason to doubt our story when we explain it to them.'

For a long, breathless moment she waited for his reaction, feeling the tension scream along the muscles of her neck and arms, down her stiff legs. Was this how a hunted animal felt, poised for flight in that instant of sighting a predator?

'You may be right,' he said at last, though his tone told her just what he thought of that possibility. 'Or it may be easier to arrange a divorce.'

She shrugged. It didn't matter to her, so long as the necessary steps were taken to release her from this marriage. Even now she found it hard to believe that she'd been married all this time without knowing it.

And the thought of being legally bound to Stavros Denakis… She shuddered. Once, if her secret fantasies were any indication, she would have thought it a dream come true to be wed to him, the handsome, dynamic man who'd rescued her. But that was before she knew what he was really like. How cold and hard and cynical.

'I don't care. Whatever the lawyers think will be quickest. Have you contacted them yet?'

'So eager to escape our union?' Sarcasm edged his voice and twisted his lips.

She shrugged, trying to focus on anything but his proximity and the sparks of awareness exploding through her. He's a bully, she reminded herself. An arrogant, egotistical jerk.

Yet there was something about him that made her long for his tenderness. Like the single, gentle touch of his lips on hers that had stolen her breath and sent trails of fiery heat twisting through her four years ago. The brief formalities had finished and the marriage celebrant had looked expectant, reminding them it was traditional to seal the nuptials with a kiss. She'd looked up at this stranger, watched his eyes darken almost to black. His head had dipped, he'd wrapped an arm round her shoulders and another round her waist, gently, careful of her bruises.

And he'd taken her to heaven. Just for the few moments their lips had clung. His embrace had tightened protectively, pulling her into his comforting warmth and solid strength. The world had spun away as her eyelids fluttered shut and she'd given herself up to the surprisingly delicate caress of his lips against hers.

The kiss had ended suddenly. He'd stared down at her, his brows angled together like now.

Then he'd looked puzzled. Now his expression was harder to read. But instinctively she knew that anger and distrust were there, hidden by his shuttered expression.

'I've already contacted my legal staff,' he said brusquely, 'and they're investigating the quickest way to achieve a legal dissolution.'

He turned away, pacing towards another huge window, and Tessa's knees turned to trembling jelly as relief flooded her. She'd been so wound up with tension from confronting him that now it was an effort to stand. She reached out a hand to a suede club chair against the wall and slid into it, grateful that his attention was fixed on the view rather than her. She leaned forward, bracing her hands on her thighs and taking a deep breath.

'It may take some time. They may need to check some matters where the wedding took place.'

That would delay things. After a bloody civil war, the tiny South American country was still barely functioning.

'Do we really need to wait that long?'

He swung round to look at her, his face an impenetrable mask. 'If we want to do this properly it must be legally binding. I want no loose ends.'

No mistaking the chill in *that* tone. If her muscles hadn't already liquefied into a palsied mess, she'd have stiffened at the icy contempt that laced his words.

'That's fine by me.' She turned her head and stared across the spacious apartment to the cluster of comfortable sofas on the other side of the room. Anything to avoid meeting his disbelieving gaze.

'And I will have an additional agreement drawn up.'

'Yes?' Tessa followed the swirling design on the sofa's upholstery with her eyes as if it were the most important thing in the room.

'It will provide you with a settlement, on condition that you speak to no one, especially members of the Press, about our marriage. *And* that you renounce all further claims to my property.'

He thought she wanted his money. He'd made that abundantly clear last night. Even so it hurt to hear it again, the accusation in his tone.

'Whatever you say,' she said wearily, leaning back in her seat and wishing he'd take his suspicions and his acid tongue and leave her alone.

'No arguments? No negotiation on price?'

'No.' She flicked him a glance then turned away. 'I'm sure you've already calculated to the last cent exactly how much you're worth, and how much my silence should cost. Why would I quibble with an expert?'

And besides, she wouldn't touch his money. But there was no point telling him that. He'd already tried and judged her in his mind. He wouldn't believe any protestation that all she wanted was to go home.

She started at a shadow of movement close beside her. It was him, looming over her. His features dark as a thundercloud. His eyes sparking an unmistakable warning.

He really *did* move with uncanny silence.

She tried to push her way up from the seat but his hand on her shoulder held her still. His grip seared through the thin cotton of her T-shirt like a brand.

'Don't play games with me.' His voice grated low and threatening, raising goose-flesh on her arms. 'You'll come out the loser.'

'I'm not playing games.' She was too weary to try shrugging out of his heavy grasp. Her burst of defiance had melted away as if it had never been. This last bout of illness really had taken its toll. She had no stamina left.

'I was just about to ring the Australian embassy in Athens to get their help in sorting out a divorce or an annulment or whatever.'

'That won't be necessary.' His dark voice came from above her. 'My legal advisors will organise everything.'

'And will they organise my flight home to Australia too? Or am I allowed to do *that* for myself?'

One look at his face told her the sarcasm was wasted. His

expression was stern and his eyes shone with a fierce light that sent a jolt of anxiety right to her core.

Then his lips curved up in a smile that owed nothing to humour. It was too…carnivorous. Too dangerous.

'There is no need for a return flight. You won't be going anywhere till this is resolved.'

CHAPTER FOUR

'ARE you threatening to keep me a prisoner here?'

Again that baring of strong white teeth that made her shiver. For all his careful control, Tessa sensed a latent barbarism in him, hiding just below the surface.

'Let us say instead that you'll be my guest.'

Stay here, in his home? The idea was too appalling to contemplate.

'And if this takes a long time to finalise?' Surely nothing involving lawyers and courts happened quickly.

He shrugged, lifting his hand from her shoulder. But still he stood too close for her to feel safe. 'I think I can manage to accommodate you for the duration.'

He had to be kidding. Her eyes widened as she looked up at him and saw not a trace of humour in his steady gaze. Only the smug satisfaction of a man who held all the cards.

He was serious! He really meant to hold her here.

'You have no right.'

'On the contrary, I have every right to ensure my privacy and protect my family.'

And he thought that by imprisoning her here indefinitely he could do that? As if he *could* keep her against her will. There must be multiple exits from the property and ways to seek help. Her eyes flicked automatically to the phone on the other side of the room then up to his hard face.

Then she remembered her passport, so conspicuously missing from her belongings when they'd been returned to her.

'What did you have in mind? Tying me up so I can't run away?' Bravado hid the shreds of fear evoked by the memory of real captivity all those years ago.

'Don't tempt me.' He leaned in towards her, his hands resting on the arms of her chair, trapping her. His dark face was pure threat and his voice a rumbling whisper that abraded her skin. 'The idea has a certain undeniable appeal.'

This close she could see that, despite the mocking tilt of his mouth, his eyes blazed with something other than fury. Something that told her he was picturing her bound and vulnerable, completely at his mercy. And the image pleased him. Tessa's eyes widened.

In that moment he looked like a man who didn't give a damn about right and wrong, about common decency or even the law, if they came between him and what he wanted.

Tessa shuddered, aware now of the hot, musky scent of his skin enveloping her as he thrust his face close to hers. The fierce heat of his powerful body, pushing her back in the chair. The skittering, swirling sensation in the pit of her stomach.

It had to be fear. It couldn't be excitement.

She felt his breath warm on her face, heard the soft sound of his steady breathing, a contrast to her own ragged gasps. He was crowding her. His head and shoulders blocked the room, his face filled her vision.

Her gaze dropped from his, latching instead onto his mouth. So determined, so hard, so close to hers. The whirl of tension in her belly quickened as his lips parted a fraction. She dug her fingers into the suede upholstery.

He couldn't mean to…

Thought was suspended as, unbidden, the memory surfaced of this man's lips moving against hers. Of the giddy excitement and sudden desire his caress had evoked. Of the yearning for more.

Tessa's eyelids flickered as he dipped his head and a charge of pure energy pulsed between them. Only disbelief prevented her succumbing to the mad impulse to give herself up to the seductive, beckoning darkness. To invite the warm weight of his lips caressing hers.

Anticipation was a palpable force, thudding through her bloodstream. It heightened her senses so she trembled as she inhaled the hot male scent of him, already shockingly familiar to her. She was attuned to the steady rhythm of his breathing, aware when it notched up a fraction. She sensed the surge of power through his body as he leaned closer.

And, to her shame, she awaited that moment with trembling expectancy. All she saw, heard, breathed was him, the man she told herself she hated.

Her quivering body proclaimed her a liar.

Hard hands grasped her cheeks, tilted her face up, aligning it with his. There was nothing gentle about his hold or the look on his harsh granite face.

Nothing except the way one thumb caressed her cheek.

She couldn't prevent the shuddering sigh that escaped her lips as she felt the heat of his skin against hers, the tiny, rhythmic movement that awoke a tide of flooding awareness, tingling through her body.

Her eyelids drooped.

'Oh, you're good.' Stavros' voice was a whispered skein of rich sound, brushing across her nerve ends. 'Surprisingly good.'

For an instant his hold tightened, then his hands dropped away and he straightened.

Shocked, she felt her eyes pop open, taking in the twist of his mouth, the narrowed stare that flashed a message of anger and disgust.

What had happened?

'Do you think I'm naïve enough to be gulled by a woman such as you? Even if you have improved your acting skills over the last couple of years?'

She flinched as the words bit into her flesh and deeper, into the tender, unprotected part of her where her last hopes and secret dreams lay hidden.

He slashed them as ruthlessly as he'd lacerated her self-respect. In one moment of temptation he'd revealed her weakness—one she thought she'd buried forever.

And she loathed him for it.

Shame seared her as sanity returned in a rush. What sort of woman had she become? She'd conveniently forgotten that he was engaged, committed to another woman.

Unbelievable!

Embarrassment heated her cheeks as she remembered the way she'd succumbed to the promise, the expectation of his lips on hers. Desires and fantasies she'd thought long-banished had swirled to the surface and reduced her to a wanting, waiting victim.

But she refused to be anyone's victim, ever again.

'You need have nothing to do with *a woman such as me* if you'd let me be on my way.' Tessa's heartbeat thudded unevenly, belying her bravado.

'You think I should relent and trust you?' His expression of haughty disbelief sat far too easily on that arrogant nose, that judgemental jaw. Tessa found herself grinding her teeth.

'No, no.' He shook his head as he smiled in spurious amity, his voice a deep, caressing purr. 'I'll trust you just as far as I could toss that delectable body of yours. Definitely not out of my sight. You'll stay where my security staff can keep you monitored at all times.

'You made your intentions abundantly clear when you chose the night of my betrothal party to announce your presence. Maximum disruption, maximum impact, maximum financial benefit to you.' He counted the points off on his fingers as he paced before her.

'It's a simple equation. And an ugly one.' That cold smile turned cruel as he stopped to pinion her with his laser-bright glare. 'Don't take me for a fool. You did your homework and decided to arrive, unannounced, in the hope of squeezing me for a substantial settlement. But you chose the wrong man. I can't be blackmailed.'

No trace of a smile now. His face was grim, harsh, absolutely forbidding. Despite her indignation, a trickle of fear slid down Tessa's spine.

'But it wasn't intentional. I didn't plan it that way.' In response to his aggression her voice was breathless and uneven. She leaned forward, hands gripping the arms of her chair as if she could absorb some of its stolid strength to help face him down.

'Of course you planned it.' His abrupt slashing gesture was violent. '*You* were the one who staged the dramatic entrance. You could have contacted me any time in the last few years and I'd have arranged to end the marriage.'

She shook her head, careless of the loosening hair that splayed around her neck and shoulders.

'No, I couldn't. I wasn't free to travel. I didn't even realise who you were or that you were alive until a couple of days ago.'

For years she'd lived with an awful sick feeling in the pit of her stomach whenever she remembered that day in San Miguel. His sustaining arm round her shoulders as they drove away after their 'marriage'. The warmth in his smile as he spoke of safety, a hot bath in a clean hotel and a meeting with embassy officials once they got safely over the border on the strength of his passport and money. And then…nothing. Just the hollow emptiness of being told there were no other survivors of the explosion.

His brows arched in wordless disbelief.

'It's true.' She shot to her feet, hands clasped in unintentional supplication as she faced him. 'I didn't escape from San Miguel like you did. I've been in South America for the last four years.'

Stavros rocked back on his heels as shock ripped through him. He was prepared for some concocted story but not this. This was outrageous.

For so long he'd believed her dead. He'd promised to rescue her before the country erupted into civil war. Yet he'd failed abysmally when a mortar had blasted the street apart as they drove to the airstrip.

With his investigation of a possible new emerald mine complete, he'd been preparing to leave when his driver told him about a foreign girl held in the local gaol. No tourists came to this backwater, not even intrepid backpackers. Even *he* had encountered difficulties travelling in the remote region. She'd been locked up as a suspected rebel sympathiser. But everyone knew she was innocent, stupid enough to be robbed of her passport and unlucky to fall into the hands of the police chief who had a violent reputation and a penchant for a pretty face.

Stavros' visit to the gaol had confirmed the truth and he'd vowed to rescue her. Just one look at her frightened, desperate face as she'd shivered in that filthy cell had convinced him he couldn't leave her behind. What else could he do? They were the only two foreigners within hundreds of kilometres. She had no other hope of escaping before the looming civil unrest erupted into a full-scale bloodbath. If that didn't finish her off, the brutality of her gaolers soon would have.

With his money and influence, there'd been no protest to him removing his 'wife' from the danger zone once she was under his protection.

But the scenario she'd just raised, of her trapped in that war-torn country, was unthinkable.

Stavros turned on his heel and paced across the room, avoiding her upturned face with its false mask of innocence.

An icy finger stroked down the back of his neck at the possibility he'd abandoned her, alone, to face that bloody conflict. His own severely concussed state when he finally came to after the blast, the identification of the dark-haired woman in jeans right beside the ruined vehicle, the official pronouncement of death counted for nothing in the face of that possibility.

'It's not true.' His voice was husky as he turned to face her. It couldn't be true.

She'd survived and escaped over the border. She'd appeared now simply because she'd finally realised who he was and how much he was worth.

'Yes, it is.' Her quiet conviction would have rocked him if he hadn't known better. But he had personal experience of grasping women and the lengths they went to for money.

'If you'd been missing all this time there would have been searches, official enquiries, *something*. Your family in Australia would have been worried and contacted the authorities. They'd have tried to trace you in South America.'

And that would have led them surely to him, the man who'd apparently last seen her alive. The man whose name was on her marriage certificate.

Slowly she shook her head. 'No. I don't have a family. There'd have been no enquiries.'

'No family at all?' How very convenient.

'My mother is dead and I never knew my father.' She wrapped her arms around herself as if cold. 'I don't have any siblings and my mother was estranged from her family. I don't even know where they live, or if I have grandparents still alive. When I get home, that's what I want to do—try to locate them.'

Her lips twisted in a way that evoked a pang of unwilling sympathy. But Stavros wasn't easily convinced by a tale of woe.

'So why didn't you escape when you had the chance?' he challenged. She hadn't stayed to help in the devastation left by the blast. She must have been long gone by the time he surfaced, wounded and disoriented.

She looked up at him, her eyes wide and pleading. 'I came to the next day, in a village miles away in the hills. I'd been rescued by a stranger.'

'A stranger?'

'Sister Mercedes. I lived with her for the past few years.'

A nun? She was asking him to believe she'd been living a life of unblemished innocence with a nun all this time?

His shout of laughter echoed in the quiet room as the un-accustomed tension drained from his taut shoulders.

Tessa Marlowe wasn't such an accomplished liar after all. She'd overplayed her hand with that particular fabrication. Living a life of virtue with a holy sister for four years.

Next she'd claim to be a virgin!

If he'd been in a more generous frame of mind he'd have given her a lesson on not gilding the lily.

'It's true!' She stepped in front of him, her chin tilted up and her hands stretched out as if pleading. A nice touch. She looked gorgeous with her eyes wide and her soft lips parted. So brave and vulnerable.

'We stayed in the mountains, where it was safer. I tried to cross the border once, later, but my guide was shot and wounded. It was just too dangerous.'

'That's enough.' He turned away, unwilling to hear any more of her lies. Each untruth from those beautiful lips sickened him.

Strange, he should be inured by now, after three grasping stepmothers and a legion of women vying for the position of Mrs Stavros Denakis. Lies and half-truths, manipulation and greed, there was nothing new here.

He strode to the door and yanked it open.

'Save your breath.' He speared her with a furious glare. 'You'll gain nothing with this pretence of innocence.'

Yet as he left the room and pulled the door shut behind him, Stavros felt an unfamiliar twinge of doubt.

Just as well he was too intelligent, too experienced to let it sway him.

Stavros stood alone in the dusk, watching the lights of a passing vessel in the bay. The intense quiet was like a benediction after the hours spent farewelling guests. It had taken most of the day, but then this was an important occasion: the merging of two significant families. And, his father had reminded him wryly, traditionally a time for rejoicing.

As if there'd be any celebrations while his wife was still on the premises.

Still his wife.

Still a threat, a potential embarrassment, a conundrum he hadn't resolved.

Stavros wasn't used to unresolved problems. And this particular problem threatened to take far too long to fix.

Preliminary enquiries by his staff confirmed that ending the marriage wouldn't be quick. Already his patience had been tested to the limit, having to house that conniving female on the premises. The knowledge that he was obliged to keep her for any length of time made his blood boil.

His hands tightened into fists at the thought of her.

All those hours today he'd stood beside Angela, politely chatting to family and friends. He'd been close enough to feel the heat of his fiancée's body, to experience an anticipatory surge of physical desire for the woman he was going to wed. The woman he'd chosen as much for her stunning looks as her character and breeding.

Yet he'd felt nothing. No flicker of heat. No hint of sexual anticipation.

Damn. He couldn't even enjoy the ripe promise of his fiancée's body. Not with this imbroglio looming over him.

Having a wife was death to a man's libido.

But his lack of response wasn't the worst of it. All day he'd been haunted by the memory of emerald eyes, of another woman, who stirred his blood in a way he couldn't explain. Even in his fury he couldn't dismiss the raw attraction for her that welled from some dark, hidden place inside him.

What was it about her that crept under his guard every time? He couldn't put his finger on the trigger that sparked such a traitorous response in him whenever he spoke with her, looked at her, even *thought* of her.

Asto kalo! He needed to focus instead on his beautiful fiancée. He'd chosen Angela meticulously from an army of contenders. She was elegant, clever, a woman who understood what drove him, his work and his family obligations. She came from a wealthy family and would fit into his life, give him companionship, sex and the family he'd decided he wanted.

She was nothing at all like the ragtag con-artist to whom he was currently shackled.

He swung around and headed for the house, sick of his circling thoughts.

Halfway across the wide terrace a prickling sensation slowed his step. Heat slid like an unfurling ribbon across his shoulders and down through his torso. He looked up, pinpointing instantly the shadowy figure, half-hidden by curtains at the window on the second floor.

Even at this distance he knew their eyes met. He could feel it in his slow, suddenly leaden pulse, throbbing with such force through his body. Awareness sizzled in his bloodstream, just as it had last night. Just as it had four long years ago.

Her hand reached up to grasp the drapes, fingers tightening on the fabric like a claw, as if she needed to steady herself.

So she felt it too, that preternatural awareness. He'd been

trying to deny its existence ever since he'd walked into the security block to see her and his heart had slammed to a halt in his chest.

It was something she hadn't feigned. Nor had she been able to hide it. Especially after today when she'd flagrantly invited his caress with her luscious, lying mouth and her tempting body, her sham air of vulnerability.

He strode on, determined not to let her read his reaction, the weakness thrumming through his bloodstream.

But all the time his mind revolved around the fact that he'd found a chink in Tessa Marlowe's armour.

Her weakness for him, her body's undeniably sensual response to his proximity, gave him a weapon to use against her, if he chose.

CHAPTER FIVE

TESSA slid through the crystal water, revelling in the wonderful sense of freedom it gave her. It had been years since she'd swum. A lifetime it seemed since she'd learned to float in the public pool of the small country town where she and her mother had lived for a few years. Their longest sojourn in any one place.

They'd stayed there long enough for Tessa to make friends, for the teachers to know her name. Even to teach herself to swim on those baking summer afternoons when the kindly woman at the gate had turned a blind eye to a scrap of a girl who didn't have the entrance fee.

Life had seemed promising then. As if maybe *this* time they'd make a go of it. Settle down and be just like the other families.

Of course, it hadn't lasted. But it had given Tessa a tantalising taste of what she wanted most: a home; a sense of belonging; friends who cared; maybe even a real family, who supported one another, *loved* one another.

Her mum had loved her, but in her own way. It wasn't till they'd settled in Gundagai for those two years that Tessa realised not all mothers were like hers: flighty, emotional, wonderful when she was taking her medication, but unpredictable and unreliable.

Then four years ago it seemed that fate had finally dealt

Tessa a good hand. After her disrupted schooling and years of poorly paid casual work, she'd saved enough to begin her social-work course in the next semester.

Her friend Sally had won tickets to Mexico and invited her along. It had seemed the adventure of a lifetime. That was before Sally fell in love with a tall Canadian and decided not to make the overland trek south that she'd planned with Tessa. Before Tessa had stepped off a bus, alone, in San Miguel and straight into disaster.

Tessa reached the pool's end, her hand slapping the smooth tiles. For a moment she sank under the surface. When she bobbed up again she blinked to clear her eyes and flicked her hair back from her face, wishing she could shake away the regrets so easily. On a surge of energy she heaved herself out of the water, to kneel dripping and out of breath on the sun-warmed terracotta tiles.

She froze as she registered what was before her: a pair of kidskin loafers—large, elegant, probably worth more money than she'd ever seen in one place at a time; dark trousers, surely made-to-measure, for the man who wore them was tall, towering above her. The stylish cut couldn't conceal the solid masculine potency of those powerful thighs.

Tessa swallowed, watching large hands, dusted with a sprinkling of silky black hair, flex in front of her.

He probably wanted to wring her neck. A few days ago, when she'd arrived, she'd actually wondered if Stavros might act on such a violent impulse. That was before she'd discovered the sort of man he was. Impatient, decisive, outrageous in his determination to get his own way no matter what the repercussions. Yet controlled. So controlled. Even his white-hot fury had been leashed after that first confrontation. He'd been incandescent with anger but it had morphed into a cool condescension. His superior air told her she hadn't a hope of convincing him to believe her.

Her breath sawed in her constricting throat as she gathered her strength to meet his gaze.

One hand thrust towards her.

'Here.' His rumbling voice was brusque to the point of rudeness. She felt like telling him she needed his help to stand about as much as she needed his absurd house arrest. But she guessed that if she didn't take his proffered assistance, he'd just reach out and grab her.

And she *didn't* want those hands on her body.

Electricity sparked, zapping through her as his hand closed on hers. For a shocked instant she paused, wondering if he experienced it too. Then she breathed deeply and got to her feet, letting him pull her up.

He didn't release her, even when they stood toe to toe.

Energy surged through her from where his palm touched her, his fingers engulfing her hand. She felt power judder through her body, filling her with heat and vibrant awareness. Yet despite the sun's rays she shivered.

Tessa tugged but his hold was firm, unrelenting.

Reluctantly she raised her eyes to his face. He didn't meet her gaze. Instead he surveyed her with a thorough sweep that made the blood rush to her cheeks. His straight brows were drawn together in a sleek line of disapproval. His nostrils flared as if in distaste and his mouth flattened out in a grim line.

What had she done wrong now?

'You said I could use the pool.' The words burst out, breathless but defiant. Now his guests had gone she'd been permitted the run of the villa's public areas.

So long as she didn't attempt to leave. Though it had been his absolute certainty that she couldn't escape, rather than any threat, that had persuaded her escape would be a wasted effort. Those grim-faced security men had a lethal professional air that was completely convincing.

Slowly his gaze swept back up her, from her trembling

legs, over her cotton shorts and tight black tank-top, heating her as it went, till fire sparked and swirled in her abdomen. It was like a physical touch, evoking an instant, eviscerating response. To her shame it wasn't embarrassment she felt now.

Again she pulled and this time his fingers eased their grip, allowing her freedom.

'Of course you may swim.' His voice was cool, dismissive. He arched one eyebrow as his grey eyes met hers, holding her where she was just as easily as if he still touched her.

He had the autocratic air of a man used to compliance. To people obeying him without question. It would give her pleasure to show him she wasn't one of his lackeys.

And yet she stood, mesmerised by a glimpse of something in those steely eyes. Something that unnerved her. Something more complex than anger.

'But there's no need to swim in your clothes.' This time his deep voice held a rough note she hadn't heard before. 'Get a swimsuit from the pool-house next time you want to use the pool.' It wasn't an offer. It was an order.

Stupid embarrassment curled within her. So she didn't have a swimsuit. That wasn't the end of the world. She had nothing to be ashamed of. Nevertheless she shrank as his eyes flicked ruthlessly over her wet body, dismissal clear in his tight expression.

No doubt it pained him to see even his unwanted guest looking so dishevelled. He probably mixed with only the most beautiful people. He was used to the manicured perfection of Angela Christophorou.

Tessa wrapped her arms defensively round herself and turned away, searching for the towel she'd left somewhere.

She told herself it didn't matter that she had no airs or graces. No glamour. Yet a forbidden discontent gnawed at her. A fleeting longing for what she'd never had.

She'd seen Stavros and his fiancée together in the distance

only this morning. He'd held her close, his arm embracing her protectively. Lovingly.

And Tessa had had to turn away from the sight as sharp, lacerating pain clawed at her insides.

Stavros watched her pluck a towel from a sun-lounger. Her movements were jerky, abrupt, as if she was nervous.

He speared a hand through his hair in frustration. Never had a situation spun so far out of his control. Never had he lost command of his own emotions! He was livid, but whether at himself or his unwanted wife, he wasn't sure.

Shock had blasted him as he read the investigators' report. It confirmed Tessa Marlowe hadn't been safe with her family these last years, or decadently profiting from her looks at the expense of some man. Instead she'd been scraping a precarious living in a third-world country racked by poverty and civil war.

Because *he,* Stavros Denakis, had failed her.

It was a powerful punch to the gut, knowing he'd been safe when she wasn't. No matter that he'd crossed the border by the skin of his teeth, with severe concussion and a fractured collar-bone. Nor that everyone had believed her dead.

His stomach roiled. Even the knowledge that she was on the make, angling for an undeserved share of his fortune, didn't lessen his discomfort.

No wonder she was so desperate for cash after the privation she'd endured. *Sto Diavolo!* That also explained her fragility. She looked as though a gust of wind would knock her down.

Yet that didn't impede the rush of raw lust he experienced whenever he saw her. Nor did the fact that he was honour-bound to another woman. It was irrelevant that there was no emotional bond between him and Angela. He'd given her his promise.

As he'd promised to protect a defenceless stranger with eyes like gem-fire four years ago.

Stavros swallowed down the bitter knot that rose in his

throat. He shouldn't feel this blood-hot craving for another woman. It made a mockery of his plans, his self-control, his very honour.

Seeing Tessa Marlowe in those ragged shorts and ill-fitting top should have emphasised how little they had in common. How distant she was from his ideal female: voluptuous, perfectly groomed and easy on the ego.

Yet the sight of her, in wet clothes that clung like a second skin, dried his mouth and froze his body. The too-tight top emphasised the surprisingly lush curves of her breasts. Her streamlined body shouted a feminine allure he was powerless to resist. Even the thick rope of dark hair, sliding over her back as she dried herself, mesmerised him.

He itched to reach for her, shape her delicate curves, caress those high, pouting breasts that would be a perfect fit for his hands, mould her tiny waist to his touch.

After just a few days of decent food there was a change in her. A rounding-out of that sleek body and a new spark of vitality. Both served only to highlight her allure. *And his guilty attraction.*

Stavros clenched his hands. Only this morning Angela had left for northern Greece and family commitments. He'd stayed behind to untangle this marriage. Yet here he was, rooted to the spot, mind atrophied by the rhythmic swipe of lush towelling over Tessa Marlowe's bare legs.

What sort of man did that make him?

Tessa wrapped the thick, oversized beach towel around her trembling body. She was chilled to the bone, scared by her reaction to Stavros Denakis.

She was right to be wary, right not to trust him. But why couldn't her brain override her body's pathetic yearning? He despised her, he was planning to marry a gorgeous sophisticate who had to be a complete polar opposite to herself. Yet still she couldn't squash that flicker of excitement whenever she felt his eyes on her.

No, not a flicker. A blaze of self-destructive passion—for what she could never have and should never want.

For too long she'd fantasised about this man, building him into a hero, a Prince Charming, because she needed to believe in *something, someone* who could comfort her when the fear crowded close and sleep was impossible.

Now she couldn't shake herself of that fantasy or her longing. Yet she had to.

She straightened her spine and turned to face him.

His starkly handsome face was more than grim. Tighter, harder than she'd ever seen it. As if he'd received the worst possible news.

As if he blamed *her* for it.

A *frisson* of fear danced down her spine and she locked her knees against the impulse to retreat.

'We need to talk.' His low, rumbling voice made the hairs stand up on her neck. Or maybe it was the iron glint of his narrowed eyes. She looked down to his hands, bulging fists, and her heart dived. He was a man on the edge.

Right now she didn't have the reserves of strength to face the full blast of his fury. The fact that she didn't deserve it would be no protection from his wrath.

'I didn't think you were interested in talking,' she said quietly, with only a trace of unsteadiness. 'You don't believe anything I say.'

Tessa watched the muscles in his jaw bunch as he clenched his teeth. The pulse under his dark gold skin beat frenetically. His blood pressure must be sky-high.

'You're right. I thought your story was a ploy to get my sympathy.'

Sympathy? That was rich. He'd treated her like a leper ever since he'd seen her. But now something was different.

'So what's changed your mind?' For something had, she could see it in his eyes.

'My staff tracked your movements, right back to your first contact with the Australian embassy a couple of weeks ago.' He paused to drag in a deep breath that made his massive chest heave. 'There's no trace of you living anywhere but right where I…left you.'

Of course. He'd believe his staff, but not her. What had she expected? That he'd suddenly realised he was wrong about her? Seen past his prejudices?

As if!

'So now you know.' She shrugged in an effort to look insouciant.

Silence as his gaze held hers and the tension thickened between them.

'It's my fault.' His words were abrupt, so unexpected that she blinked, wondering if she'd heard him right.

'I should have protected you better. There was another route to the airstrip. We could have taken that.'

Tessa stared, her brain whirring in shock as she digested his words. He blamed *himself* for the explosion that had ripped their vehicle apart?

No one could have anticipated that!

A muscle in his jaw worked and tension hummed from his big frame, drawing her nerves tight in response.

'You couldn't have known about the mortars.'

He jerked his head once, emphatically. 'I should have made it my business to find out.' He took a step towards her, and then pulled up abruptly.

This close she could see beyond the blankness of his rigid control. She saw the turmoil in his eyes, the doubt and…pain?

A shaft of something sharp pierced her chest at the idea of him, the man who'd rescued her from torture and death, blaming himself for the violence of others.

It didn't matter that he'd behaved abominably ever since she'd turned up on his doorstep. Now, for the first time since she'd arrived, Tessa saw traces of the man she'd first met and admired. The strength. The unquestioning acceptance of his role as her protector. The innate decency. Some of her icy shell of self-protectiveness thawed at the recognition.

She saw past his air of invulnerability and she was swamped by the need to reassure him.

Tentatively she raised a hand towards him, reaching out to touch his arm. Then her courage failed and she let her arm drop. Far better to avoid physical contact.

'It wasn't your fault,' she whispered over a throat clogged with raw emotion. 'You did everything you could. More than anyone else did.'

Again that single abrupt jerk of the head in denial. 'But that wasn't enough.' His tone was bitter. 'I had made myself responsible for you.' He stared over her head as if the very sight of her pained him.

Perhaps it did.

Suddenly the onslaught of memory, the swirl of unsettling emotions, were too much. Tessa's knees buckled and she swayed. She stumbled a step and dropped onto a wide, padded sun-lounger, hunching forward to wrap the luxurious towelling tight round her trembling legs.

An instant later he was crouching beside her, eyes piercing as they surveyed her.

'You're ill.'

She shook her head, frowning at his concern.

'You need a doctor.'

'No! There's nothing wrong with me.' Nothing that rest wouldn't cure.

'That's not what the doctor said.' His gaze seared her and she blinked.

'You talked with the doctor about me? What about patient confidentiality?'

He didn't even bother to answer. Presumably what Stavros Denakis demanded, he got.

If she'd had more energy Tessa would have made an issue of that. But at the moment the churning mass of emotions in her stomach kept her fully occupied.

She was confused, wanting to hate this man who stomped without apology through her life, yet undercut by her weakness for him and the unexpected sight of his vulnerability. For all his air of refined savagery, Stavros Denakis was a decent man.

He simply hid it well.

He surged to his feet, drawing a cell-phone from his pocket. An instant later he was issuing directions in staccato Greek. But one word Tessa caught: Michalis. That was the name of the doctor.

'No. I told you I don't need to see a doctor again.' She leaned forward to interrupt, putting her hand out to touch his.

A bolt of sensation rocketed through her as flesh touched flesh and she gasped. The feel of warm, hair-roughened skin beneath her fingers was far too intimate.

Had he felt it too? Unerringly her gaze darted to his, to find his expression once more impenetrable. Did she imagine the flare of heat she saw there?

She whipped her hand away as if the contact scorched her, then wished she hadn't as his brows rose imperceptibly. He'd noted her reaction and no doubt catalogued it away for future use against her.

'The doctor will be here soon.' His voice gave nothing away.

There was no point in another consultation. All she needed was rest, nourishment and the medication the doctor had already provided. She was hardly some delicate flower.

Tessa notched her chin at the man towering above her. 'Then I hope you and he have a nice chat. *I* won't see him.'

For a heartbeat Stavros' expression remained stony, then, to her amazement, the corner of his mouth kicked up in the barest hint of a smile. Even that was enough to transform his face from forbidding to seriously sexy.

Tessa's heart thumped harder against her ribs.

'Don't push your luck, Ms Marlowe. While you're in my house I'm responsible for your wellbeing. I take no chances.'

Casually he folded his phone and shoved it into his pocket. He didn't move away, just stood, far too close for comfort, looming above her. His spicy masculine scent teased her nostrils.

'After all,' he continued in a musing tone, 'we don't want you claiming neglect or physical maltreatment, do we?' His gazed bored into hers and she leaned back away from him, startled by the speed with which he'd morphed from sympathetically human to sneeringly superior.

'It would be a tempting ploy,' he continued, 'but if you try it you'll find my lawyers less eager to reach a reasonable settlement with you.'

They were back to that again? The realisation was a body blow, robbing Tessa of air and cramping her stomach.

For a moment she'd thought there was a chance they might reach some kind of truce. But it seemed that Stavros Denakis' mistrust was even keener than his sense of guilt.

'You *still* believe I want your money?' She wouldn't stoop to plead her case, not when it was sure to fail. Yet she could barely credit the depth of his scepticism.

'You think I should believe you're a complete innocent because of the hard life you've led?' His dark brows rose as if in genuine surprise. 'I think not. Women are rarely that straightforward, and I think most people would see your first act as a free woman, in flying across the globe to find me, rather telling. Of course you're after a slice of my wealth.'

Tessa sat up straighter, curling her fingers tight into the cushioned seat. Anger vibrated through her, making it difficult to find her voice. 'You see yourself as an expert on women, obviously. Has it ever occurred to you that perhaps, just once in a while, you might be wrong?'

His mouth quirked up in a humourless smile.

'You should have done your research before you decided to try extorting Denakis money. Though in the circumstances I suppose your opportunity to investigate me *was* limited.'

Tessa trembled with the effort of sitting there instead of surging to her feet and slapping her palm across his arrogant, self-satisfied face. Or of kneeing him hard in the place most precious to his inflated masculine ego.

'I suppose you consider all women are after you for your looks and your money,' she said quietly. 'What a shame to have such doubts about your own worth. To be always wondering about people's motives.'

His brows snapped together and something dangerous sparked in his eyes. He didn't move yet somehow his bulk seemed larger, more menacing.

'I'm used to women throwing themselves in my path,' he murmured in a provocative tone designed to raise her blood pressure. 'Of them flaunting their bodies and trying to insinuate their way into my bed. Of the coy looks and the brazen invitations.'

He shrugged and his gaze slid, assessing, over her body, firmly swathed in towelling. Nevertheless, she felt his scrutiny as if no barrier protected her from him. It was like a physical caress and she knew he was recalling her reaction when they'd been together in her room and she'd thought he'd kiss her. She hadn't been able to hide her anticipation, her breathless eagerness.

Heat bloomed in her throat and rose to scorch her cheeks. Darkening eyes met hers and held her gaze.

'I have a particular expertise when it comes to women who extort money via marriage.' His mouth thinned to a brutal line. 'I met the first of my stepmothers when I was ten. The second when I was sixteen. The third at twenty-two. Not one was the genuine article, a loving wife who cared for her husband and new family.' He bit the words out with such hatred that she winced. 'And each was more selfish and mercenary than the last.'

He swung away to stare out to the dark blue Aegean lapping around the pier at the foot of the gardens. In profile his jaw was tight, his mouth hard and his eyes curiously blank.

He looked more alone than anyone she'd ever seen.

A whisper of unwilling sympathy softened the stiffness of Tessa's rigid frame.

'I've seen it all,' he said, his voice a low rumble that against all reason created a twist of compassion deep inside her. 'I've witnessed every ploy, every parody of affection. Women who abuse their bodies in order to look the part of a fantasy lover. Women who care more about their manicure than their promises of fidelity and love. Women whose sole aim is a life of luxury, even if they have to sell themselves to achieve it.'

His deep voice grew harsher and Tessa shuddered at the wealth of cynicism there. She'd never persuade him she was different. Why did she even want to try?

Tessa pushed herself up from the seat, turning to leave, and found herself facing the black-clad man who'd interviewed her the night she'd arrived. His face was devoid of betraying emotion. Yet his waiting stillness sent trepidation tingling down her backbone.

'Kyrie Denakis.'

Stavros swung round, his expression abstracted. But instantly she sensed him focus on the newcomer, shoving other thoughts to one side.

'Ne?'

The word was a signal that unleashed a rapid spate of Greek. Tessa had no hope of understanding what was said. Yet, despite the way both men avoided so much as a glance in her direction, as the tension built to a throbbing pulse in the heavy atmosphere, she *knew* this was about her.

She tugged the thick towel closer to counteract the increasing chill in her veins.

Finally there was silence. Long. Threatening. Pulsatingly alive with unspoken accusation.

Stavros asked a single curt question, heard the response and then flicked a stabbing glance at Tessa. Gone was all trace of vulnerability. Of humanity. This man was icily controlled. Eyes bright as lasers sliced through the veneer of her composure, cutting to the bone.

Involuntarily she stepped back.

The security expert spoke again in an earnest undertone. Stavros gave what could only be an order, and the man turned and strode towards the house.

Stavros pulled his phone from his pocket, turning away and breaking eye contact. Instantly the clenching pain in her chest eased. She drew a shaky breath, filling her lungs with oxygen. She had to know.

'That was about me, wasn't it?'

At the sound of her voice Stavros froze in the act of hitting the speed dial for Angela's number.

He was leashing his temper only with the greatest effort. He'd never been so close to losing control.

Fury shuddered through him, like the aftershocks of an earthquake. A quake that had shattered the calm when Petros had appeared with his news.

Slowly he lifted his gaze. She was staring up at him, wide-eyed and apparently hesitant.

Something turned inside him, a shifting, burning ball of wrath that curdled his stomach and sent darts of fire through his bloodstream. He trembled with the force of it.

The face of innocence. That was the image she projected. And it was pure sham. Was there any female, anywhere, who was honest to the core? Who didn't live by guile and greed?

His jaw tightened as he battled for calm.

This close he could see her eyes dilate with fear as she registered his simmering anger. She took a step back and then suddenly she was teetering on the pool edge.

With one swift stride he closed the space between them, hauling her away from the edge and setting her aside. His grip was hard and his fingers flexed against her slick skin. Instantly he withdrew, dropping his hands and taking a few paces away so he was beyond temptation's reach.

It would be totally understandable if he closed his hands round her shoulders and shook her senseless for the damage she'd caused by her selfish actions. But he wouldn't give in to the primitive impulse.

'What makes you think we were discussing you?' Even to his own ears the question was thick with menace.

'I… It was obvious.' Her voice was a husk of sound but there was no satisfaction in the knowledge of her fear. At the moment he felt nothing short of blood would appease his anger.

It was a good thing for Tessa Marlowe he was a civilised man.

'The Press know about our marriage.' He stared down at her, looking for a flicker of knowledge or excitement. Something that would confirm her guilt. 'The story is about to appear in every news-sheet and scandal magazine.'

'How…?'

'I thought you could tell me that. Surely it suits you to have the marriage common knowledge?'

'No! No, I wouldn't do that. I *didn't!*'

'And you expect me to believe you?'

'No,' she said, shaking her head. 'I know you won't believe anything I say. But that doesn't alter the fact that I've never spoken to a journalist.'

'Spoken, written to, contacted. The semantics don't matter. The fact remains that you're the one to gain.'

He shoved his hands into his trouser pockets, ignoring the instinct to reach out and force the truth from her.

'Your staff can tell you there haven't been any phone calls to the Press and I haven't posted any letters. As for email—I don't even know where your office is so I haven't accessed the net.'

She had a point. Petros had assured him she'd been incommunicado. But that didn't clear her. She must have found some way to get a message out.

'Unless you think I've been sending semaphore messages from my bedroom window?'

'There's no need for sarcasm,' he growled.

'Well, how *did* I talk to the Press? Have you even considered the possibility it wasn't me?'

'No one else has the same motive,' he countered. 'You're the one looking for bargaining power to get my money. But I won't be blackmailed.'

'If it's such a good story, surely it's worth something? Why not question your employees? Plenty of them knew I was here. One of them—'

'Silence!' With an abrupt gesture he cut her off. 'Don't try to shift the blame to them.'

'You can't ignore the possibility.'

'I can and do. I know all the staff here intimately.' He'd grown up with most of them. He'd trust them instead of her every time. 'There's no question that they'd leak the story. Besides,' he paused, 'you might have let the news out before you arrived here.'

'You're so trenchant in your suspicion!' She tilted her chin, her eyes blazing fire at him.

'And you're so predictable.' A pity. He wondered what it would be like to meet a woman who was everything Tessa Marlowe claimed to be.

The idea was a chimera, a mere fantasy.

He'd wasted enough time mulling over this. He drew his phone from his pocket and turned away.

'Don't worry, Ms Marlowe. I'll find out exactly how and when the news was passed on, and by whom. Then there'll be a reckoning.'

He was already looking forward to it.

CHAPTER SIX

THEY were still there.

Tessa stood hidden in the shadows as she peered out of the window to the road that ran beside the Denakis compound. News vans and cameramen clogged the area. Telephoto lenses focused on the gates and periodically swept the windows on this side of the mansion.

The paparazzi had surrounded the place two days ago, as soon as the news broke. Ever since the world had discovered the head of the mighty Denakis clan had married an unknown Australian.

The media had reached fever pitch, speculating about how one of Europe's most successful men came to have both a wife and a fiancée. Tessa had cringed at the few seconds' footage she'd seen on television last night, of a grim-faced Stavros leaving a sleek limousine to stride past shouting reporters on his way into a city building.

He'd looked suave, sexy, powerful, and so forbidding he might have had murder on his mind. In all honesty, Tessa couldn't blame him for his fury. She'd erupted into his life at the most inopportune time imaginable.

She was glad she hadn't come face to face with him since he'd accused her of selling her story. He'd been incandescent with rage. Enough to make her wonder if he was the type to resort to violence. After the media circus of the last couple of days, she dreaded to think what sort of mood he was in now.

Tessa craned her neck to see the side-gate. What would the photographers do if she managed to get past the guards and escape? Could she stroll past, pretend she was a stranger, an anonymous tourist?

The early-morning sun glinted off a massive camera lens as it swept the perimeter wall and her heart sank.

No. No chance she could sneak out unnoticed. Which left her few options.

She'd rung the Australian embassy. To her surprise there'd been no bar on the call, though she suspected it would have been different if she'd tried to ring a Press agency. Their advice had been to stay where she was.

Tessa had hesitated, about to blurt out that she no longer had her passport. That she was virtually a prisoner. But something had held her back. Perversely, the Denakis villa had become a sanctuary. The lassitude she'd felt for weeks was fading but she wasn't up to organising her future or coping with the full onslaught of the Press. It was easier to stay as Stavros' unwanted guest for the moment than summon the energy to leave.

Abruptly she swung away and strode to the stairs. She needed air, and the grounds of the estate were private.

She was skirting a wide tiled living area on the ground floor when a sound made her pause. To her left a door opened and there stood Stavros, watching her. As if he'd known she was there.

Tessa shivered at the intensity of his gaze, wishing she could walk on and pretend she hadn't noticed him. But inevitably she faltered to a stop.

He wore a dark suit of tailored perfection. A snowy white shirt, a silk tie of deepest crimson. He looked the epitome of the successful businessman.

Yet something about the expression in his eyes, the way he held himself, hinted at another Stavros Denakis: a man of primitive power, as if the trappings of the tycoon were a camouflage for something far more elemental. And far more dangerous.

It seemed to Tessa, as she absorbed the sight of him, that the authority he wielded so effortlessly had little to do with his business or his enormous wealth. It came instead from his steely determination, his innate confidence and the aura of unvarnished masculine power that even the best tailoring couldn't tame.

Brute strength had never appealed to her. But, as her pulse tripped up a notch and her breathing jagged out of rhythm, she faced the fact that this man affected her in ways she couldn't begin to understand.

'Ms Marlowe.' He inclined his head just as if they'd parted on polite terms.

'Mr Denakis.' She met his gaze, refusing to be cowed.

One corner of his mouth tilted briefly, creating the merest hint of a half-smile that surely couldn't be as compelling as she imagined. It was gone in a flash, leaving him looking more sombre and forbidding than before.

'We need to talk.'

Said the spider to the fly. But there was no avoiding his invitation. Tessa pushed her shoulders back and walked towards him, grateful when he stepped to one side so she could enter the room. The more space she had around this man the better.

'Take a seat.' The sound of his deep voice so close behind her made her start forward. Quickly she took in the huge study with its state-of-the-art technology, its wide, gleaming desk and the huge black leather chair behind it. No way was she sitting meekly in the visitor's seat drawn up before the desk. Instead she swerved and headed for the comfortable chairs positioned around a low table. She sank into one and carefully placed her hands on its arms, striving to look composed.

He didn't settle opposite her. Instead he stalked to the full-length windows, staring for a long moment at the view of sky and sea. When eventually he turned to face her his expression was unreadable. The light behind him threw his features into shade. But the set of his shoulders was rigid. *Not* a good sign.

'I owe you an apology,' he said abruptly.

Tessa wondered if she'd heard him right. She never thought she'd hear an apology from Stavros Denakis. Yet he sounded so uncomfortable it must be real.

'So you *believe* me?'

'I know you didn't leak the secret of our marriage to the Press.'

She leaned back in her chair. *At last.*

'So who did?'

Restlessly he shifted. 'A waiter employed on a casual basis by the caterer hired for the engagement party. We have proof, direct from the journalist involved.' Icy disapproval edged his voice but there was no mistaking the underlying blaze of heat.

Tessa shivered. Journalists were notorious for protecting their sources. She didn't like to think about the sort of pressure Stavros had brought to bear in order to get this information.

'And the waiter? What's happened to him?' She should be glad the real culprit had been identified. Yet she couldn't help wondering what price he'd paid for his actions.

'No more than he deserves.' Stavros paused. Was he relishing the thought of vengeance? 'He'll never work in his field again, not here in Greece and certainly not with any top-quality international firm.'

Tessa froze at his merciless tone. He really was ruthless.

'You think I'm too harsh?'

'No. Yes. I think…it will be difficult for him to start again somewhere else.'

His wide shoulders rose in a dismissive shrug. 'He should have considered that before he breached the trust of his employer, and his client. If he wanted money he should have worked for it honestly, like everyone else.'

There was no answer to that.

'He was looking for easy cash,' Stavros continued, slowly pacing away from the window towards her. 'Just like women who see marriage as a convenient way to get rich.'

Tessa's breath hitched. Not again. She'd thought they were beyond this.

Now he loomed beside her and she sensed disapproval in every line of his hard, muscular body. She shot to her feet, unwilling to be at such a disadvantage.

'So, you know I didn't tell my story to the Press and yet you insist on believing I'm here for your money?'

'It would take much more than that to convince me you're the *innocent* you claim.' His grey eyes fixed on her, probing, as if to uncover her every secret.

If only she could persuade him she *had* no secrets. Her life was an open book. She was sick of his doubt and his disapproval. They hammered at her incessantly.

'It must be a very cold, bleak life, living with constant suspicion.' She glared up at him. 'I just hope your fiancée has a warm disposition to balance it.'

'My fiancée?'

His voice held an odd note. Instantly she knew she'd overstepped some unwritten mark. Perhaps women such as she weren't allowed to mention Stavros Denakis' bride-to-be.

'Yes, your fiancée.' She met his stare unflinchingly, watching his eyes darken to the colour of a winter storm.

'Your attempt at humour is misplaced,' he growled. 'Or were you, perhaps, trying to rub salt into what you hope is an open wound?'

'I…' She frowned, trying to follow his logic.

'Come, come, Ms Marlowe. No need to be coy. You must know I *have* no fiancée. Not any more.' He leaned close, intimidating just with his presence. 'And I think we can both agree that's down to *you*.'

Tessa saw his long fingers flex and bunch as if he sought a physical outlet for the wrath bubbling inside him. Carefully she shuffled back a pace, but not enough to escape if he reached for her. Her mouth dried.

'I didn't know.'

He tilted his head, assessing her words. 'It's been in all the news reports. Along with every aspect of my personal life the Press can get its hands on.' He didn't bother to conceal his bitterness.

'I don't speak Greek. I didn't know,' she repeated, numb with the knowledge that he was right. This was *her* fault. If she hadn't come here…

'I'm sorry.' She gripped her hands before her and stared up into his dark, disapproving face. 'Was there no way you and your fiancée could—?'

'What? Maintain our engagement while I was still all too publicly married to you?' His eyes flashed derision. 'I think not. Even if Angela had been willing, I couldn't have expected it of her. I ended the engagement the day the Press got the story.'

The look in his eye told her the experience hadn't been pleasant. And that he intended to exact revenge for it.

Her pulse skittered as anxiety took hold, deep in her belly. She felt like a fish trapped on the end of a line, drawn closer and closer to its doom.

His lips curved up in a smile that held no warmth at all. Tessa had to lock her knees against the impulse for instant flight as she read the searing intent in his eyes.

'So that leaves just the two of us,' he murmured, pacing closer. 'How cosy. Just me and my lovely wife.'

He reached out and, before she could escape, closed hands as unyielding as iron around her shoulders, drawing her inexorably towards him.

She looked up into those cold eyes and knew real fear. Try as she might, she couldn't wrench out of his grasp. Perhaps that was what he wanted: an excuse to constrain her even more tightly.

Instantly she stilled, her heart pounding and her breathing rapid.

'That's better,' he purred in a voice of rough silk. 'It's nice to see you so biddable.'

He slid one hand across from her shoulder to her collarbone, so his palm rested flat on her bare skin and his fingers splayed across her throat. It was the lightest of touches but she sensed that his hold would tighten if she made a single unwary movement. His touch felt hot enough to brand her skin.

'Now,' he mused, a dark smile hovering at the corners of his mouth. 'The question is: what should I do with you?' He paused. 'No suggestions?'

Tessa's throat closed.

His fingers moved, stroking the length of her throat in a feather-light caress that drew all the strength from her. Then he was cupping her jaw, his hold light but unbreakable.

'It's a shame I have an appointment with my legal team in Athens. But you'll understand I don't want to miss that.' His voice held an edge of mockery. His thumb slid across her bottom lip in a parody of a lover's caress and Tessa felt an answering tug of sensation deep in her belly.

'But don't fret, wife.' He leaned close so that his breath feathered her skin. 'I'll think on the matter and we can talk about it when I return.'

Tessa had seen the helicopter leave an hour ago. She knew Stavros had gone, and yet it had taken her this long to summon the strength to leave her room.

He'd been toying with her; he wouldn't really resort to violence. Yet she shivered as she remembered the velvet menace in his voice. There'd been such fury in his eyes, in his very stance. And a smouldering desire that scared her more than the rest put together.

Even now, knowing she was alone, she paused at the bottom of the staircase, listening before she ventured out into the gardens.

That was when she heard it. A rapid click-click-clicking. No voices, no movement, just the quick sound of…what?

Intrigued, Tessa walked down the broad ground floor corridor till she came to a large tiled living area. Then she faltered. On the other side of the room a man sat beside a carved table, intent on moving counters on a wooden board.

His appearance snagged her breath. The wide shoulders, the arrogant tilt of the head, the massive frame. All were familiar; the family resemblance was so strong. Yet this man was much older than Stavros Denakis. His hair glinted silver, his face was lined with age. He'd been ill too; his cheeks were sunken and his shirt hung loosely.

The clicking stopped and his gaze lifted to meet hers unerringly, as if he'd known all along that she hovered there at the perimeter of the room.

'*Kalimera, Kyria Denakis.*' He inclined his head, still watching her with eyes that looked startlingly familiar under strong black brows.

'I'm sorry,' she murmured. 'I don't understand Greek. What did you say?'

His mouth twisted up in a movement that could have signified either welcome or impatience.

'Good day, Mrs Denakis,' he rumbled, his voice like a husky echo of Stavros at his most superior.

His words, as much as his tone, welded her to the spot, horrified. She opened her mouth to deny the title he'd given her, and then shut it again.

Technically he was correct. She *was* Mrs Denakis.

The realisation shuddered through her.

'I've been curious to meet you,' he continued as if he hadn't dropped a loaded bomb at her feet. He paused. She had the impression he was sizing her up every bit as ruthlessly as Stavros had.

'Allow me to introduce myself. I'm Vassilis Denakis. Your father-in-law.'

Stavros strode from the helipad up to the house, glad to be on his own territory again. The Press were like midges, buzzing about incessantly, stalking his every move, snapping their cameras in a feeding frenzy. As if they'd get any more fuel for their stories from him!

He was used to Press attention, had grown up with it. But this was testing his patience to the limit. Even his minders, the best in their profession, had their hands full fending off the boldest of the paparazzi.

If there was one thing he didn't enjoy, it was feeling that he wasn't in complete control of a situation. It didn't help to know that the current mess was the result of his own actions four years ago.

Add to that the long-distance discussion he'd just had with Angela's uncle about financial compensation for the broken engagement… No wonder he was seeing red.

The score he had to settle with Tessa Marlowe grew larger by the hour.

At least the meetings with his lawyers and PR staff had been straightforward. They might be agog with curiosity but they were professionals and they kept their tongues between their teeth while they did what he decided had to be done. There were no impertinent questions about how he'd got into this situation, just a focus on how to get out of it.

He shoved open the exterior door. What he wanted now was a hot shower and a decent brandy. Or a workout in the gym to slough off some of his tension.

He felt strung too tight. Annoyed at being the victim rather than the victor.

It wasn't what he was used to.

He'd almost reached the stairs when a murmur of voices reached him. The hoarse grunt of his father's laughter.

What was the old man doing here? He'd been obstinate about remaining across the bay in the old-fashioned villa his great-great-grandfather had built. Had he finally agreed to do as Stavros wished and move in permanently?

Stavros doubted it. His father was as stubborn as a mule.

He swung round and headed to one of the sitting rooms, following the sound of counters clicking rhythmically round the tavli board. It seemed his father was entertaining one of his friends. But why here?

Stavros quickened his step in response to a premonition of trouble. He felt it in his bones.

He rounded the corner of the room and pulled up short, the breath seizing in his lungs.

Hell and damnation! He didn't believe it.

But it was true.

The old man was playing tavli with his daughter-in-law. With Stavros' wife. With the treacherous little con-artist who'd caused such disruption. Who'd made him a laughing stock and planned to fleece him if she could.

They made a cosy pair, their heads close together over the board. So very domestic!

Stavros clenched his hands in fury, repressing the sudden desire to stride across the room and smash the board to the floor. To pull that designing female to her feet and shake an admission of guilt from her lips.

For a moment he indulged himself, imagining the horror on her face. There'd be no more coy glances and pretended outrage. Even though she hadn't fed the story of their marriage to the Press, he knew one thing: the cause of this whole disaster was sitting there, large as life, pretending interest in his father's obsession for tavli.

He speared his hand through his hair, striving for some shred of his usual iron control. But it eluded him.

The old man was lapping it up. Look at him! He even smiled at her, nodding approvingly as she moved her pieces around the board.

There was no fool like an old fool, was there? He should have known his father would take one look at Tessa Marlowe and succumb to her air of fragile independence. To her perfect face and luscious, treacherous mouth. He'd listen to her honeyed lies and believe what she wanted him to believe.

Vassilis Denakis had a soft spot for gorgeous young women. Three times he'd been taken in by them, going so far as to marry them, not seeing beyond their flattery or their willingness in bed to their selfish avarice.

It had been left to Stavros to see what sort of women his father had chosen to foist on the family. To suffer the appalling wait until the scales dropped from the old man's eyes as infatuation waned.

Stavros had learned his lessons about women early. It would take more than Tessa Marlowe's delicate beauty or bright eyes to make him forget them!

Grimly he stalked across the room, wondering just how far she'd inveigled her way into his father's favour.

'Having fun?'

Tessa's hand spasmed at the sound of that deep, mocking voice and the dice clattered to the board. She jerked her head round to find Stavros pacing slowly towards her.

Like a rabbit caught in a spotlight she stared, unable to move, as he halted beside her. Close enough for her to see the rise and fall of his muscled chest under the silk business shirt. For her to discern the steady tic of his pulse at the base of his throat, where he'd tugged open his tie and undone the first couple of buttons.

But it wasn't the proximity of his powerful body that snared her gaze. It was the predatory intensity of his eyes. They were simmering hot, glazed with strong emotion.

And they scared her.

His eyes were dark charcoal-grey as they flicked from her face, down her body and back up again. That look grazed her skin, heating it to unwilling awareness. But more, his gaze seemed to devour her. As if she were some tasty morsel served up for Stavros Denakis' delectation.

She shivered as the hairs stood up on the back of her neck, then watched his slow, deliberate smile as he held her eyes with his.

He knew how he intimidated her, and he enjoyed it!

Her hands were clammy with sweat as she sat up straighter, ready to defend herself. He might be bigger and more powerful than she, but she'd fight tooth and nail if she had to.

'The girl learns fast,' said Vassilis Denakis from across the table. 'With practice she'll be an adversary to be reckoned with.'

Tessa shot a surprised look across the table at the unreadable face of the old man who'd been a surprisingly pleasant companion this afternoon. He was watching his son intently, as if to assess the impact of his words.

'It wouldn't pay to underestimate her,' he added.

'There's little chance of that, Patera. A man would be a fool not to treat this woman with the utmost caution.'

Despite her anxiety, Tessa felt her hackles rise at being referred to as if she weren't there.

'I've enjoyed our game.' She turned to Vassilis Denakis with a tentative smile, knowing that their quiet interlude was over. 'Thank you for teaching me.'

'The pleasure was entirely mine.' He inclined his head in a

courtly gesture that surprised her. It seemed that the Denakis men could be charming if they chose. Or at least this one could.

She was all too conscious of Stavros looming beside her, vibrating with impatience and something darker, more dangerous, that she wanted to avoid at all costs.

'I'll look forward to our next game,' the old man added.

Tessa flicked an urgent glance at Stavros, but his attention now was on his father, his brows slightly raised.

It was her chance to get away from the fraught atmosphere and the giant of a man who menaced her with barely an effort. She pushed back her chair, careless of it scraping across the broad tiles.

'If you'll excuse me, I'll leave you two to catch up. I need to go and…'

'Yes, Tessa?' Stavros' deep voice stroked across her skin, like rough suede. 'What is it that you must do?'

She tilted her head up, up, till she met his eyes and managed not to flinch as his scorching gaze captured hers.

Desperately her heart thudded out a panicky beat. She swallowed hard and smoothed her clammy hands down her cotton trousers.

'I have to go and wash my hair.'

Let him make what he liked of that!

She rose, concentrating on trying to appear confident and at ease. All the while her nerves jittered in distress.

With a nod to Vassilis Denakis and a cold stare at his son, she forced herself to walk slowly across the massive room and out towards the main foyer. It wasn't until she was halfway up the impressive staircase that her resolve splintered and she stumbled into a run, desperate to reach the sanctuary of her room.

Tessa was in the bathroom, unpinning her hair, when an atavistic presentiment that she was being watched shivered through her. Her hands froze, the weight of her hair sliding down in a lopsided tumble, as the skin of her neck tingled and she spun round to face the door to the bedroom.

He'd discarded his tie and jacket, rolled up his sleeves and stood, one forearm propped casually against the door jamb just above his head. But there was nothing casual about the look on Stavros Denakis' face. It wasn't a scowl, yet she felt disapproval emanate from him in waves. And more. Something urgent and powerful that made her want to shrink away. But there was nowhere to run. She was trapped.

Tessa's pulse notched up as she fought the primitive impulse to flee. The only way out was past him and the look in his eye told her he wasn't ready to let her go anywhere just yet.

What did he want?

'I see you've been making the most of my hospitality.' His voice was like liquid mercury: heavy, silky smooth and deadly.

Tessa didn't answer. What was there to say? Instinctively she knew that any response would only goad his temper.

Her gaze skittered from the taut curve of his bicep, flexed as he leaned against the door jamb, to the grim line of his mouth and up to the deep glitter of his eyes. They all proclaimed one thing: threat.

Slowly, almost idly, he slid his arm down from the door and straightened, stretching his shoulders back as if to relieve some unseen tightness there.

Tessa felt her eyes grow huge as she watched him.

He was the ultimate predator.

And yet…to her horror she felt a trickle of purely feminine appreciation of the ultra-masculine picture he made.

'Don't think you can take advantage of my father.' This time there was no silk in his tone. It grated, harsh and uncompromising.

'I didn't try to—'

'And don't make the mistake of believing I'm not awake to your games.'

He took a single stride into the room as he spoke, filling it with his alarming presence.

'I never even—'

'This is between you and me. Just the two of us. No one else.' He closed the distance between them so she had to lift her chin to meet his look.

'Is that understood?'

She nodded once, jerkily, not trusting her voice now she was close enough to see what was in his eyes.

Her pulse leapt up into her throat, drumming a tattoo so fast and urgent that her breathing clogged. She opened her mouth and sucked in a laboured breath and saw his gaze drop to her lips.

Instantly heat flared deep in the pit of her belly. Her chest felt impossibly tight as those gleaming eyes watched her draw another shuddering breath.

She had to get out of here. She was claustrophobic with him so close. Somehow he was stealing her air, making it impossible to breathe.

She took a shuffling step to one side, and was rewarded by the sight of his long arm reaching out in front of her, his hand splaying against the mirrored wall beside her, blocking her exit.

'Please.' Reluctantly she lifted her eyes again to his, facing that searing intensity with barely a flinch. 'Let me go.'

Silence pounded between them. A silence filled with the ponderous thud of her out-of-kilter pulse and the rasp of her uneven breathing.

'Of course I'll let you go, Tessa.' His lips tilted in the slightest of smiles. The effect was a carnivorous baring of strong white teeth that sent fear coiling tight round her lungs.

'It will give me the utmost pleasure to be rid of you,' he murmured. 'But not…quite…yet.'

Mesmerised, she stared as those fierce eyes grew closer. His hot breath seared her cheeks. His lips eased back from their feral snarl.

She knew she had to push him away. Force herself into action.

Instead she waited, breathless, as his mouth dropped to cover hers. The heat of his body surrounded her and she gave in to the inevitable.

CHAPTER SEVEN

His mouth was hard, demanding, devouring.

Exciting.

In a single possessive movement he hauled her close, one arm wrapped round her waist, pulling her into his body, his other hand buried in her hair, holding her still while he angled his face over hers.

She was utterly defenceless against his strength and erotic expertise.

He kissed as if this was war, as if he were some conquering general, intent on total subjugation. His lips dominated her until, with a muffled protest, she opened her mouth for him.

Dazedly she realised that was a mistake. On a surge of triumphant power his tongue took possession of her, demanding submission.

In that moment she was lost.

Stavros filled her every sense. The smoky musk scent of his skin rose in her nostrils, like heady temptation. His throaty low growl of satisfaction as she yielded echoed in her ears. The sensations of his hard body were all round her, crowding closer as if he could meld them into one. His hand cradled her skull, fingers rhythmically caressing her hair. The taste of him, so addictive, filled her mouth and left her craving more.

Her hands were trapped against his solid chest, the thin silk of his shirt no barrier to the scorching heat of his torso. She felt his heart thud strongly, rapidly, beneath her palm. She wished she could feel his flesh bare against her hand.

Desire surged through her, igniting a fire that licked at her from the inside. This was insane, self-destructive, and utterly unstoppable. She'd dreamed of his possession for so long. Somehow, it seemed, her body and her mind had already accepted his ownership, and colluded to short-circuit the urgings of common sense.

Darts of sensation plunged through her sensitised body. A swirling coil of need circled in her abdomen. It seemed as if her breasts swelled against the hard muscle of his upper body and her nipples tingled.

His tongue lunged and curled around hers, till she had no choice but to respond to its seductive, outrageously demanding dance.

For a moment he stilled, as if surprised as she caressed his mouth with hers, tentatively mimicking his actions. His whole body hardened, even the pulse of his heart kicked out of rhythm for an instant.

Then he gathered her even closer, dragging her up, almost off the floor, and in against his blazing heat. His hunger was raw and blatantly obvious. His body throbbed for her. She felt his arousal surge against her and something melted inside her, hot and sweet like molten sugar.

Restlessly she shifted against him, and was rewarded when large hands clasped her bottom and hauled her higher, till that potent heat was against her very core. Urgently she slid against him, eager for the new sensations he awoke in her.

She felt edgy, hungry. Desperate as she'd never been for a man.

His kiss grew ravenous as he thrust hungrily into her mouth. Now she held him, her hands clamped in the softness of his black hair as she revelled in his possession. In the awe-inspiring power of this man who held her so effortlessly, and drew her to a fever pitch of need.

She tilted her head, the better to accommodate him. He ravaged her mouth with a thorough expertise that left her reeling and craving more.

Her lips were throbbing when he finally dragged his mouth from hers. He was so close her universe was encompassed by dark, glittering, febrile eyes, and by the feel of him clamping her against him, as if, for him too, close wasn't close enough to satisfy the storm of escalating desire.

His chest heaved against her and she heard the rasp of uneven breathing, his and hers together, as they strove for oxygen.

Silence stretched between them as Tessa tried to control her whirring thoughts. To make sense of what had just happened and to decipher the expression on his face. She could read heat, emotion, intensity. And what else?

Suddenly she shivered, as cold reality slipped in. He was her enemy. The man who hated her, believed her to be a mercenary liar.

The man who until just a few days ago had been engaged to another woman.

Hell!

Blood sizzled under her skin as heat washed through her. How could she have forgotten? How could she have let him—?

'You really are something,' he murmured, still holding her up against him so she couldn't find the purchase to move away. His hands had slid to encircle her waist and she fought the flutter of traitorous excitement at the sensation of his proprietorial touch.

'You're either the best actress I've yet come across, or...' His words trailed away as slowly, oh, so slowly, he lowered her. Each centimetre was a lesson in the power of desire and the magnitude of her guilt. For even now Tessa couldn't repress the tremor of excitement that rippled through her as she slid down his hard body. His unashamedly aroused body.

Her eyes squeezed shut in dismay at her own appalling weakness.

'Or,' he continued, leaning forward to whisper in her ear, his lips teasing erotically against her skin, 'you really are panting for it. Which is it, Tessa? Are you so desperate for me that you'll spread your legs right here? Right now?' His hand slid up her back in a parody of the caress she'd felt as he kissed her.

Or perhaps that earlier embrace had been false too. Maybe it had all been a con. A sick, twisted game that Stavros played just because he could. Because he held all the cards in this particular deck.

Because he'd seen her vulnerability and decided to use it against her.

For a nauseating moment she wondered if he realised just how inexperienced she was, and whether that gave an extra fillip to his monumental ego in seducing her so quickly, with such insulting ease.

With a violent jerk she wrested herself away from him, arms flailing and legs kicking. She jammed her knee up in what should have been a crippling blow, but he was too fast, deflecting her with a swift sideways movement. She slithered from his grasp, stumbling because her knees were so unsteady, her legs boneless.

He reached for her, grabbed at her waist just as she slipped off balance, but she shoved his hands away.

'Let go of me!'

Horror lent her strength to escape his grasp and lurch through the doorway into the huge bedroom. She needed air or she'd be sick, she knew it. After the closeness of the bathroom, scented with the heady perfume of arousal, of warm, wanting flesh, the breeze coming through the open bedroom window was like returning sanity.

'Don't touch me!' Tessa spun round as she sensed him emerge from the bathroom.

He paused in the doorway, body tense as he surveyed her.

Nevertheless, she backed a couple of surreptitious paces away from him. Out of reach of those long arms.

'You didn't mind me touching you a moment ago,' he drawled and she avoided his eyes, concentrated instead on the bunched muscles of his forearms as he planted himself, legs wide and arms akimbo, facing her.

'That was a mistake. You forced—'

'No! Don't hide behind more lies, Tessa.' He paused and she watched, mesmerised, as his chest rose and fell with a mammoth breath. 'I didn't force you. You responded to me. Willingly. Eagerly.' He took a step towards her and her heart thudded painfully.

'Wantonly.'

'No!' Her gaze crashed into his, and she felt herself sinking again. As if he only had to stare at her with that glint in his eyes for her to lose all sense of right and wrong. For her to abandon herself to the most dangerous of follies.

'No.' This time it was a whisper, almost a plea, as she strove for control over a body that still craved the magic of his touch.

'Yes.' His eyes narrowed as he swept a comprehensive glance over her. From her trembling legs to her heaving chest. From clenched fists to her peaked nipples, still pouting against her bra, as if eager for his caress.

Tessa shuddered, wondering just how *wanton* she looked. Was her arousal so obvious? She felt torn in two, needing the safety of solitude, yet still battling the shreds of desire.

'I don't want you,' she lied through her teeth.

'That's not what your body tells me.' There was grim amusement in the slight curve of his mouth and his self-satisfied tone. Damn him!

'I don't care what you think. I don't want you near me.'

The engagement might be at an end—for now, but surely emotions couldn't be turned off so easily. If Stavros and Angela had been close enough to consider marriage they must care deeply for each other. The fact that Stavros could use Tessa for sheer physical pleasure while he was still linked, emotionally at least, to another woman was a deliberate insult.

She watched his mouth thin to a straight, disapproving line and aimed for the jugular. 'What about your ex-fiancée? I'm sure she wouldn't like to know what you've been up to so soon after jilting her.'

He closed the gap between them, till his massive chest, his formidable shoulders, blanked out the rest of the room. Tessa felt the anger roll off his skin in waves to encompass her. It was all she could do to stand her ground, not give in to the impulse to scurry away from his intimidating presence.

For she knew there'd be no escape. Not unless he permitted her to go.

Reluctantly she tilted her chin and looked right up into his set face. The force of his glare almost knocked her off her feet.

'Are you trying to blackmail me…*again?*' His voice was a silky whisper that sent fear scudding down her spine.

'I…' She swallowed, trying to moisten her mouth. 'I've never tried to blackmail you. But you seemed to have forgotten—'

'Oh, no.' His look burned her, bright and keen as a blade slicing right through her defences to leave her utterly vulnerable. 'I forget *nothing*. Especially the way you've plotted to use me for your own ends.'

She opened her mouth but his voice stopped her, its icy cadence freezing her blood.

'Believe me, it will be best for you if you never mention Angela in front of me again.'

Tessa wrapped her arms tightly round herself, hunching in against the chill fury of his lashing tongue. He blamed her for everything.

And why not? It had been her naïve stupidity in coming here that had sparked this disaster. Now Stavros' enmity seemed fathomless.

Because she had injured the woman he loved.

The realisation cramped Tessa's stomach in a jolt of pain, as if she'd received a body blow.

'But since you're so concerned as to mention my ex-fiancée,' he said ponderously, his voice deepening to a low rumble, 'I should tell you, our connection has been completely severed.

'So you see,' his voice continued, silkily taunting, 'in the circumstances, there's no reason why I shouldn't have a taste of what you're so freely offering.'

The heavy silence between them was shattered by her gasp of indrawn breath.

'They say variety is the spice of life and I have to admit to being…intrigued to see just how far you'll go in your attempts to carve out a slice of my money.' He paused and the silence between them grew thick and fraught with barely curbed emotions.

Stavros looked down at the woman before him and tried to seize control of his wayward imagination.

'Are you just a tease? Or are you honest enough in this at least? Will you follow through with what you just offered and give me your body?'

Deliberately he lashed her with words that stripped this extraordinary attraction between them down to its most basic, brutal level. For, to his dismay, he discovered he was fighting himself as much as her.

He needed to dismiss the flood of emotion that threatened to drown him when he held her close and inhaled the sweet scent of her. To cut away the illusion that this was something different, special. That Tessa Marlowe was somehow unique.

Yet, despite his bluntness, his deliberate callousness, it wasn't working. Still he was in her thrall, bound by the memory of her ripe sweetness and her clumsy eagerness.

No! It was a ploy. Her stock-in-trade. A trick to dupe him.

And yet his thoughts centred inevitably on the memory of that lush, seductive mouth opening for him, inviting him inside. Of the heady lust that had blasted through him from the moment he'd hauled her close and discovered just how delicious it was to hold her in his arms and hear her soft mews of pleasure. As he plundered her mouth in precisely the way he wanted to take her body. As he felt her undeniable response.

The primitive surge of ownership he'd experienced as he spanned her tiny waist with his hands had rocked him to the core. The soft, decadent caress of her waist-length hair had almost unmanned him.

He needed her so badly it was a physical ache. Even now. Even knowing what she was.

'Don't.' The single word seemed torn from her, as if she was in pain. She closed her eyes as if she couldn't bear to face him.

And he was the biggest fool of all for believing that, even for an instant. Hadn't he learnt anything from his father's mistakes? No way was he going to repeat them.

If only he had some defence against the feelings this woman aroused in him. If only he could relegate her to a simple legal and financial problem, instead of a living, breathing woman who insinuated herself into his brain, into his very bloodstream so that he could never be free of her.

Sto Diavolo! She even kept him awake at night with the hottest erotic dreams he could remember.

His voice was harsh with self-loathing as he continued. 'But perhaps we should negotiate your terms first. That way there will be no misunderstanding when it comes time to settle your account.'

Her eyes snapped open, drowning emerald-green, to stare up at him with such a welter of emotion that it stopped him in his tracks.

He read anguish there. Pure, unadulterated pain so raw and

real that something deep in his chest clamped tight in response, constricting his lungs till he could barely breathe.

Her skin paled and her mouth stretched into a taut line of suffering.

'Tessa…' The hoarse whisper was his, dragged from him as her pain reached out and lanced his body.

How could that be?

Could he really be falling for her act of innocence?

He shook his head, not believing the strength of the sudden doubt that assailed him.

Still her gaze held his, making him feel like a lout who'd taken out his wrath on an innocent child or some defenceless animal. As if *he* was the one at fault here. Not the conniving, deceitful, sexy woman before him.

The woman who was like no female he'd ever held in his arms. The woman who carved right through his logic and his ego, who threatened his ordered world in a way he'd never imagined possible.

'I want you to leave now.' Her voice was light and toneless, so insubstantial that he almost didn't catch her words over the relentless drumming of blood in his ears.

She blinked away a glaze of tears, yet her eyes were still overbright as she stared up at him.

He didn't budge. But after a moment he felt unaccustomed heat crawl up his throat.

With her angled chin, her drawn face and her steady look she radiated determination, elegance. Class.

To his astonishment uncertainty gripped him. Was it possible he'd got it wrong? That her motives weren't mercenary after all and she'd been telling the truth? For a moment Stavros felt his conviction crack, a lifetime's lessons totter and sway.

Then sense reasserted itself. He had to hand it to her, she was the best he'd come across, in a lifetime littered with women on the lookout for an easy life.

'And why should I leave? I *am* your husband. Which means I have certain *rights.*'

The convulsive movement of her throat drew his gaze. That was when he saw the frantic beat of her pulse at the base of her neck. Instantly guilt speared him, as if he really had hurt her.

'Because I want you to.' She hesitated. *'Please.'* For a moment longer she held his gaze then she swung away towards the window, her movements jerky. She kept her back to him but he saw the way her shoulders hunched high as she hugged her arms round her torso. 'I can't—'

'Enough!' He cut across her. Already she'd managed to make him feel like a predator, a villain attacking some wounded innocent. He didn't need to hear any more. He didn't *want* to hear any more.

He turned on his heel and marched to the door, pulling it shut behind him as he reached the corridor. There he stood, unmoving, trying to make sense of what had just happened as the blood roared like a wild thing in his ears.

He didn't know which disturbed him more—the ravening hunger for Tessa Marlowe that grew with every moment he spent in her company, or the way she made him feel he was in the wrong. As if she was the innocent in all this.

Either alternative was appalling. Both indicated just how badly out of control he was.

And that had never happened to him before. Ever.

CHAPTER EIGHT

STAVROS left her alone after that. Each day he departed early, striding long-legged and confident to the helipad. No doubt he slept like a log, satisfied that he'd put her in her place.

Meanwhile Tessa still bore the brunt of that appalling scene. She relived the exquisite excitement she'd felt in his arms and her utter horror when he'd confirmed what he *really* thought of her.

She'd love to land one good punch on him. To inflict a fraction of the raw pain he'd dealt her. As if she'd even make an impact on that hard, muscled body!

That hard, hot-as-sin body. She remembered how it felt to be embraced by him. To be kissed as if he wanted to devour her, draw her in so tight that their bodies became one. She was ashamed to admit it but the liquid heat still burned like wildfire whenever she remembered.

Years ago she'd put Stavros on a pedestal, thought of him as a knight in shining armour who'd given his life to rescue her. In her fear and homesickness, she'd focused all her thwarted emotions, her desire on him.

Now she faced the uncompromising reality of Stavros Denakis the ice-cold tycoon, the angry man using his sharp tongue and quick mind and physical strength against her. Yet still she was hampered by remnants of fantasies where he was *her* hero. Where he protected *her.*

Where he wanted her for himself.

Perversely, she could understand his viewpoint. He thought he was protecting his family and the woman he loved from a scheming witch. Tessa had seen the bone-chilling blankness in his eyes when he'd spoken of his stepmothers. No wonder he was slow to trust and ready to doubt.

It didn't excuse his appalling behaviour. Her skin crawled when she remembered his savage accusations. Yet through her misery and anger she felt a sneaking compassion for him. What did that say about her?

She needed to forget that and focus on the future. On a time when Stavros would be just a memory, not…her husband.

Tessa slumped against the fine-grained leather of the limousine's back seat, barely registering the quaint beauty of the coastal town through the tinted windows.

She should be ecstatic to escape the confines of the villa, if only for an hour and under the chaperonage of Stavros' burly minders. Instead she fought back despair.

Her life was a mess. Leaving Greece wouldn't solve her problems. She didn't have a place of her own in Australia. She'd have to find somewhere to live while she job-hunted and fended off the Press. And that was after she sorted out the legalities of this marriage. How she was going to do that when she never again wanted to face the man who was her husband, she didn't know.

She squeezed her eyes shut and drew a deep breath. No point in rehashing history. She'd do better to prepare for this upcoming interview with Vassilis Denakis. The summons from Stavros' father had come just thirty minutes ago.

The question was: why should her father-in-law want to see her again?

Stavros paused in the courtyard of the house where he'd grown up. He remembered when it had been home, filled with warmth and laughter. With its own unique perfume: sea salt and the jasmine his mother always wore.

The memory seemed so real. Then he realised it *was* real. The scent of jasmine came from a vine in the corner.

He frowned. When had the old man had it planted? His last wife, the icy Nordic beauty with a heart as cold as an empty wallet, had decreed the garden was old-fashioned and *passé*. She'd ordered it be dug up and paved.

He pushed open the door, reluctant to enter. Not because of ghosts. But because he'd prefer *not* to see his father make a fool of himself over another beautiful woman.

Tessa had come here every afternoon this week. Sometimes the old man returned with her to share a meal with Stavros, talking about the business with a vigour that had been missing since his last stint in hospital.

Stavros had intended to ban her visits. Yet when his father spoke about her he sounded like his old self. Before illness and money-hungry women had taken their toll.

His father had a new lease of life and it was at least partly due to Tessa. Stavros was torn between wanting to thank her and wanting to lock her away where she couldn't interfere. Somewhere she couldn't play on the emotions of a man with weak lungs and a penchant for a pretty face. Where she'd be utterly at Stavros' mercy.

Heady anticipation coursed through him at the image of Tessa locked in a bedroom, awaiting his convenience. It evoked intriguing possibilities. His blood heated to sizzling awareness at the mere idea.

He frowned as he walked down the hall. He'd avoided her ever since that mind-blowing kiss had obliterated his control. One kiss had him desperate for another taste, eager for the exquisite release that he knew instinctively she could give him.

He'd been betrayed by his own body. By lust for a woman he *knew* was just as calculating as his stepmothers.

No wonder his fury had known no bounds and he'd lashed out, throwing all his guilt and disillusionment into the barbs he aimed at her. He'd been almost beyond reason, scared above all by his own weakness.

His gut clenched hard in shame. There was no excuse for the barbaric way he'd treated her.

He'd avoided her lest he find himself unable to behave like a rational, civilised man. Where Tessa Marlowe was concerned he'd developed the instincts of a Neanderthal. It was ownership he felt, possession he wanted.

She thought him an uncouth lout. Yet better that than have her discover her power over him. All she had to do was turn her beguiling green eyes on him, soften her pouting lips just so, or let him close to her delectable body and he was lost, raw instinct taking over from careful logic.

Sto Diavolo! He almost wanted to believe in her. He was a fair way to becoming a fool. Just like his father.

Carefully Tessa poured the rich, pungent coffee from the beaker into two tiny cups.

'It looks good,' Vassilis said from the other side of the table, leaning forward to inspect it. 'Much better than that first attempt of yours.'

She laughed, her lips stretching easily into a smile that only a few days ago had felt stiff and uncomfortable. Her first effort at making Greek coffee had been disastrous. Now, after days of practice, the brew was drinkable.

'Nothing could be that awful.' She passed him the *demitasse* cup with the obligatory glass of water and sat down. 'Well, taste it. Or do you think it'll poison you?'

Steely dark eyes under black brows looked up at her and for an instant her breath snagged. Sometimes the similarity between Vassilis Denakis and his son was devastating. The same eyes, same large frame, same decisiveness and impatience. She wondered if, like his father, Stavros had a softer side, carefully hidden from public view.

She'd never get close enough to find out. A pang of crazy regret sheared through her at the knowledge.

'Not bad,' Vassilis said, cutting across her thoughts. 'In fact...' His brows rose as he stared over her shoulder, his words petering out.

A prickle of sensation lifted the hairs at her nape and a tingle of hot awareness spread over her skin. She'd only ever felt that when Stavros looked at her.

He was here, his hot, disapproving gaze ready to devour her, his tongue primed to lash at her feeble defiance. No doubt he'd decided it was time to take her to task for daring to visit his father without express permission.

Her mouth dried. Was she ready for the confrontation?

'How nice to see the family gathered together. The pair of you look quite...domestic.'

Despite his sarcasm, a tiny thrill shivered through Tessa at the very masculine sound of that voice. As always, her body revved into heightened awareness when he was near.

'Stavro! What are you doing here?' Vassilis asked. 'Is something wrong at the office? You're back early.'

'Nothing is wrong, Patera. I just decided to come home.'

Vassilis' rounded eyes told Tessa how rare that was. She braced herself and turned to face Stavros. Inevitably his impact, those keen eyes and the aura of energy about the man, made her glad she was sitting down.

Heat rocketed up to her cheeks as his gaze moved to her, slowed and fixed on her face, her mouth. He was remembering too. The combustible desire, the almost violent passion. That kiss. The accusations that had flayed every defence, leaving her vulnerable and in pain.

She turned her head away and sipped from her cup. Her

hand shook so she had to hold it with both hands to prevent the liquid spilling.

'Would you like coffee?' she heard Vassilis ask. 'Tessa makes a passable *metrio*.'

'No, thanks. I'll save that pleasure for another time.'

Tessa shivered as he lingered on the word *pleasure*. Unbidden, memories engulfed her of the ecstasy she'd felt in Stavros' arms, ravished to within an inch of her sanity, just by his mouth, his heat, the urgent hardness of his rampant body so close to her own.

In the silence that followed she tried to focus on the coffee in her hand, on the lovely light-filled room. But some unseen force compelled her to turn, till his darkening gaze snared hers and everything else fell away.

'I have some pressing business to conclude,' he said, his eyes never leaving hers. '*With my wife.*'

Stavros said nothing at all on the short drive back to the villa. Tessa was torn between relief at the respite and horror at the way the silence merely racked up the suspense. Her nerves were at a breaking point.

Tension throbbed between them, thick and stifling, as she remembered the last time they'd been so close. When he'd kissed her and the world had splintered into a haze of heat and passion and desire.

But instead of interrogating her about her visits to his father, or berating her again for her perceived crimes, Stavros merely stared out the window of the chauffeur-driven car. When they reached his house he escorted her through the mansion to the seclusion of his office. There he gestured for her to take a seat before the desk. This time she meekly subsided into the chair, her legs weak from reaction to the enforced proximity of the short car trip.

Hell! Where was her backbone?

'I have a document for you to sign.' His voice was clipped.

She watched him lean forward to slide some papers across the desk towards her. He didn't move from her side and the heat of his nearby body fed her edginess.

Tessa stared at the document on his desk and a sense of relief eased her strain fractionally. It really *was* a business meeting. This she could handle.

If only Stavros wouldn't loom, his presence an inevitable distraction as he stood near enough for her to breathe in the spicy scent of his skin and for her flesh to prickle in awareness.

She scowled at the papers, the legal jargon blurring as she struggled to concentrate. Out of the corner of her vision she saw his hand, large and square, reach down to place a gold pen on the gleaming desk. He wore his ring. The ring she'd carried against her heart for years. The sight of it so close sent a strange, disturbing *frisson* through her.

'For your signature.'

'Thanks.' She refused to look up at him. 'But first I'll have to *read* it.'

Was that a huff of exasperation from beside her? Frankly, she didn't care. No way was she putting her name to anything she hadn't read. Even as a way of escaping quickly from his dominating presence.

For a moment she sensed him tense, radiating impatience in a way that made the hairs rise on the back of her neck. Then abruptly he moved away.

Instantly the tension humming through her eased and she settled more comfortably in her seat.

'Of course. I wouldn't expect anything else.' His tone dripped displeasure as he strode round the desk to lean over and punch something into his computer keyboard.

Tessa stared across at him, her gaze drawn inevitably to that strong profile, the chiselled, sensuous lips. Even the frown that marred his wide brow didn't detract from his dark good looks.

A chill rippled through her as she wondered whether she'd ever be free of his magnetism. If she'd ever be able to see Stavros Denakis and not feel anything. Especially not the curling spiral of need that danced deep in her abdomen whenever her gaze met his.

He swung round in his seat and fixed her with a look. Her breath hitched and for a moment the heavy pulse in her ears blotted out his words. She looked down at the document and forced herself to concentrate.

'It's quite straightforward,' he was saying. 'And I've had the agreement drawn up in English so you'll have no trouble understanding it.'

'Thank you,' she said automatically.

He didn't deign to respond.

'Basically it's an agreement to formalise what you'll have to do to get a settlement from me. And what you *can't* do. It will be binding on both of us.'

Tessa's head shot up at that, a protest on her lips. How many times did she have to tell him she wasn't after his cash?

But the uncompromising look in those steely eyes told her he wouldn't listen. He'd never listen to anything she had to say. The omniscient Stavros Denakis had made up his mind and there'd be no changing it.

'If you turn to clause eight, I think it is,' he leaned across the desk, impatiently flipping pages until he found the right spot, 'you'll see the list of things you agree to.'

He ticked them off on his fingers.

'You won't reveal information about me to anyone. That includes information about my personal circumstances, my home, family, friends, everything right down to the design of my house and the food that's served here.'

Her eyes skimmed the text as he spoke, amazed at the level of detail. Obviously Stavros was leaving no loopholes.

'You will not discuss with *anyone,* journalist or not, the circumstances of our wedding, our married life or our divorce.'

Was that a hint of triumph she heard? He must be jubilant at the prospect of their divorce proceeding.

'Nor will you speculate in any way about me, my ex-fiancée or any aspect of my life. Is that clear?'

'Abundantly.' She flashed him a look of annoyance but he was impervious. He leaned back in his chair, obviously content that he had the situation completely sewn up.

'And just to make sure, there are penalties if you breach the contract.' He steepled his fingers beneath his chin and smiled at her. His expression reminded her of the way a wolf bared its teeth just before leaping on its prey. Her hand crept to her throat, fingers spreading defensively across her bare flesh.

Despite his air of relaxed assurance, the business tycoon managing the negotiation of a formal agreement, there was something feral about the way he watched her, unblinking. As if he was looking for an excuse to shed the civilised persona and use brute force to subjugate her.

Tessa shivered and thrust the thought aside, tearing her gaze from his and bending over the papers again.

'Turn the page over and you can see the penalties I mentioned.' No mistaking the satisfaction in his voice now.

She found the section he'd mentioned and sucked in her breath. The fines were hefty. More, she figured, than she could hope to earn in a decade.

No wonder Stavros was so pleased with himself.

'And if you keep going,' he gestured impatiently for her to turn the pages, 'there's the section you'll be most interested in. The payment you receive after you sign.'

The phone rang on his last word but he didn't move to answer it. She looked up to find him staring expectantly.

A burst of annoyance flared inside her.

'You might as well answer it. I'm not signing until I've read it all through.'

His eyes narrowed, concentrating the impact of that biting look. Tessa merely raised her eyebrows and waited.

On the sixth ring he reached out a long arm and picked up the receiver, his gaze still pinioning her. After listening for a few moments he gestured imperiously to the pen on his desk and swivelled his chair round to face his computer, the phone pressed to his ear.

It must have been important news, for within a couple of minutes Stavros was absorbed in a document on the screen before him, discussing it at length over the phone.

Resolutely Tessa turned back to the contract. Yet the soft Greek syllables, in that low, resonating voice, played havoc with her concentration.

She turned to the last page…and froze.

Eyes widening, she stared. She darted a look at Stavros but he was absorbed in his conversation, had dismissed her from his mind as if she weren't there.

Tessa's gaze dropped to the page before her and she drew a shaky breath. She'd known Stavros was wealthy, but this was…unbelievable.

For the third time she read the clause setting out the payment she'd receive if she signed. If she promised not to speak to anyone about her relationship with Stavros, and more, if she renounced all further claims on his assets.

The amount was staggering. The number of zeros in the figure sucked the breath from her lungs. It meant she'd be wealthy, securely rich for the rest of her life.

No scrimping and saving. No worry about finding a decent place to live. She'd never even have to work.

Tessa felt her eyes bulge as she read the paragraph again. And again.

Her stomach churned. It was really worth this much for him

to know he was free of her? How much money did he think she wanted? Surely even the most avaricious of ex-wives would be content with less than this.

A sigh shuddered through her as she realised what this meant. All she had to do was sign and she'd be free. The divorce would take longer, but essentially she'd be free. Stavros would no longer fear she might blurt something to the Press and he'd let her walk out of the door.

Her hand hovered over the slim gold pen.

It was what she wanted, wasn't it? To be able to go home. To get on with her life. Most of all, to put Stavros Denakis where he belonged—in her past.

Only a fool would cling to the notion he had any place in her life. Especially after the way he'd treated her.

Her fingers trembled.

She stole another look at Stavros across the wide expanse of desk. He was concentrating on the computer screen. The glower that had creased his features was gone and he looked every inch the tycoon: confident, decisive, focused. The expensive jacket couldn't hide the power of his massive shoulders, or the sizzle of energy that emanated from him as he leaned forward to type something.

This was what he lived for: his business.

What had happened four years ago, when he'd gone out of his way to save a stranger, was an aberration. An episode best forgotten.

Tessa blinked to clear her gaze as she looked back at the document before her.

She dragged in a deep breath and picked up the pen.

CHAPTER NINE

TESSA had almost reached the top of the central staircase when she heard a door slam and the sound of rapid steps crossing the vast marble-floored vestibule. Instantly she quickened her pace.

She'd done what he wanted, signed his bloody document. Now there was just one thing more she had to do: pack her few belongings and leave. With or without her passport it was time she left. This time tomorrow she'd be in Athens, organising her flight to Sydney.

Tessa turned down the corridor towards her room, trying to think about where she'd go when she landed, while she looked for a place to live.

'Not so fast.' Stavros' deep voice from just behind her was silky smooth but it held a note of warning that accelerated her pulse. He was close enough for his breath to stir her hair. Adrenaline burst into her bloodstream, fuelling an instant desire to flee.

Long, hard fingers encircled her elbow in an implacable grip. Unreasoning panic flared, made her twist in his hold.

What more did he want from her? Hadn't she done what he demanded? Surely he was satisfied now.

'Let go of me!'

'Not until I have some answers.'

His hold tightened as he marched her straight past the door

to her suite. He didn't bother to shorten his stride to match hers and she stumbled, struggling to keep up.

'You're hurting me.' His grip had tightened as she tried fruitlessly to shake him off. It was like trying to wrest off an iron manacle without a key.

'And you think I care?' His voice was grim, as if he only just managed to keep a lid on his boiling wrath. Nevertheless his hold eased. Not enough for her to tug free, but his fingers no longer bit into her flesh.

They turned into another hallway, one she'd never seen. Tessa had a fleeting impression of vivid abstract paintings on the walls and then he shoved open a door on the left, dragged her in and slammed it shut behind them.

The crash of solid timber echoed in the silence reverberating between them. Tessa lifted her eyes to his and flinched at the naked fury she found. Gone was his ice-cold mask, the steely glint that had so often sent a shiver down her backbone. Now his eyes blazed, lit by a furnace of raw emotion that blasted her to the core.

'What?' she challenged. 'What have I done now?'

She tugged and this time he let her go. Involuntarily she backed up a step, and another. His wrath shimmered in the air between them, a potent, tangible force.

He jammed his fists on his hips and stared down at her. It was a wonder that look didn't burn her to a crisp, reduce her to a pile of smouldering ash on his expensive carpet.

And suddenly Tessa had had enough. Finally, gloriously, she'd reached the absolute end of her control.

She didn't give a damn what his problem was. She didn't care what power he had or how difficult he could make her life. She didn't even care about her own sense of guilt at this ridiculous pot-boiler drama of a situation she'd landed them in. The blood sang through her body as she planted her feet wide and matched him, glare for glare.

'Go on,' she challenged. 'Spit it out.'

His eyes narrowed. A week ago, even a few days ago, she would have trembled at that look. Would have backed down and tried to find a way to escape the rage that vibrated from him. Now she almost welcomed it.

Anger rose and coiled up within her, like a sleeping dragon waking to take flight. She felt strong. Powerful. The strength of her fury blotted out everything else, even her pathetic yearning for this man.

'What's your game?' he snarled.

'I don't play games. I leave that to you.' Euphoria buoyed her as she challenged him. It was liberating, shedding that fear and those other, weaker emotions, tapping into the frustration and anger she'd reined in for so long. Releasing some of the pain of recent years.

'You can't win against me. I have the resources to squash you. Like that.' He raised a hand and squeezed one clenched fist till his knuckles whitened.

She revelled in the sight of him so clearly at the edge of his control.

'You can only win if I choose to play your game.'

'What's that supposed to mean?'

She shook her head. For an intelligent man he had a lot to learn. After the way he'd treated her he could wallow in doubt for however long it took. One day he'd realise how he'd miscalculated her motives.

He paced closer and she lifted her chin to keep eye contact.

'Work it out for yourself, Kyrie Denakis.'

A low noise, almost a growl, throbbed through the air between them. Instinctively Tessa backed a step away as the feral sound shivered across her skin.

'Why did you do it?'

'Do what?'

'*Sto Diavolo!* You know what.' He surged forward, thrusting his head towards her, like a bull ready to charge, nostrils flared and eyes gleaming with violent intent. 'The agreement: why did you do it?'

Deliberately she shrugged, trying to invest the gesture with an insouciance she wished she felt. 'I signed it. What more do you want?'

Stavros shut his eyes, giving vent to his feelings in a furious torrent of Greek expletives. The fact that his voice never rose above a whisper made the impact somehow more frightening. Despite the thrilling sense of power Tessa felt in standing up to him, caution prevailed and she paced back a couple of steps. She didn't want those hands reaching out and touching her again.

'You know what I mean!' This time his voice was a barely muted roar. 'Why did you cross out the clause about the payment you're to receive?'

'Oh, that.'

'Yes…that.'

She lifted one eyebrow in mocking imitation of him. 'Surely a man of your experience and intellect can work that one out for himself.'

'Don't play games with me, woman. What are you up to?'

'What, me? Up to something?' She shouldn't enjoy baiting him quite as much as she did. But she was only human and she was so tired of being made to feel guilty, inferior, a problem to be swept under the carpet. 'What a thing to say about your wife.'

His lips pulled back in a grimace. He looked as if he wanted to take a bite out of her.

'I'm not up to anything,' she added quickly. 'I just don't want your money. You can keep it.'

'You know the power you've given me,' he murmured, 'by excising that clause and initialling the change? I don't have to give you anything at all to buy your silence.'

'Well done!' Despite the tiny trickle of trepidation along

the back of her neck, Tessa couldn't deny herself the satisfaction of a slow, taunting hand clap. 'I knew you'd catch on eventually.'

With a single stride he obliterated the distance between them and something awfully like apprehension scudded through her. Defiantly she met his stare, refusing to back down.

'I don't know what you think you're doing—' he began.

'Oh, I know exactly what I'm doing.' Tessa's voice was firm and resolute. 'I'm going to pack my bag, collect my passport and leave. I don't give a damn about your suspicions. There's nothing more to be said between us.'

'Isn't there?' Stavros' eyes darkened to a charcoal glow, a fiercely burning stare. 'Then what about this?'

Large hands grabbed her arms and slammed her in against his body. It was hard as stone, searingly hot and pulsing with naked fury. Instinctively Tessa lifted her hands to shove him away but he stymied her, short-circuiting her self-defensive move in the simplest way.

He hauled her up on her toes and kissed her.

It was an invasion, a no-holds-barred assault on her senses. With a single guttural growl of satisfaction he tilted his head over hers, the better to pillage her mouth. One hand cradled her head and the other wrapped round her waist as he bent her back over his arm till she was no longer standing against him but clinging for support.

The bare savagery of his actions, the pure dominance of his big body crushing hers should have been the ultimate insult, a bully's way of demanding submission.

But the desperate instincts that had prompted Tessa to defy him coalesced into a single driving force. There was no yielding, no acquiescence to his rough domination. Instead the anger, the pain, the impatience morphed inside her into an escalating passion that matched his.

Her hands slid up, pushing through his hair till they grasped his skull and tugged him closer. Held him still while she met his tongue with her own and plunged into the hot, velvety recess of his mouth. She tasted the salt-sweet tang of him, his unique, tantalising flavour, and need swelled inside her. A need for more, so much more.

A moan shuddered through her. His? Hers?

Desperately she pushed up into his embrace, revelling in the hard-muscled strength of his chest against hers, the encompassing power of his arm supporting her.

This must be the most dangerous thing she'd ever done and yet she'd never felt as safe as now in his embrace.

He widened his stance. She felt his thighs surrounding her, straddling her legs, and heat bloomed suddenly, devastatingly, in the very core of her. It radiated out, melting the furious tension that had strung her so tight, till she sagged, boneless and pliable in his hold.

She trembled as he moved and his torso slid against her. Her breasts were so sensitive it felt as if he'd ignited sparks of static electricity inside her. Her nipples hardened to pebbled nubs that throbbed with need.

The hungry caress of his mouth devouring hers, the splay-fingered possessiveness of his hold, the exciting sensations as his body pressed, rubbed against hers: each one was enough to rob her of coherent thought.

His hair was the only soft thing about him; even his lips, his tongue, demanded. In response raw hunger exploded inside her. Hunger for more caresses, more sensation, more of *him*.

Blood rushed in her ears so she couldn't make out what he said, only the fact that he muttered something, the words reverberating in her mouth.

He hauled her up higher as he straightened. Yet he didn't break their kiss as he paced across the room, holding her tucked in close against him. Something bumped the backs of her legs and then she was falling, still held tight in his embrace. She landed on a mattress and for a moment Stavros' body pressed down on her. Then he rolled, drawing her with him, so they lay on their sides.

She gulped in a single deep lungful of air before his mouth was on hers again, ravaging, insistent. She opened for him and immediately the waters closed over her head, sucking her down into a flood-tide of desire.

One hand wrapped round her, holding her close while the other slipped down her back, closing over her buttock so she instinctively drew forward, against the hard length of his erection. She gasped and the sound was swallowed in his throat. He pulled her closer, intimately close, as he thrust his lower body against her.

She'd never felt this urgent need, like a drug in her blood, deafening any call to sanity, making her utterly reckless in response to the urgings of her body and the pure temptation of his.

She rocked against him, hips against hips, and again she heard it, that deep, throbbing sound in his throat, halfway between a growl and a purr.

Stavros gripped hard at her hip then slid his hand to her waist. His fingers on the bare flesh under her shirt were large and heavy and exciting. Her ancient cotton shirt was in the way as he explored higher. With a grunt of satisfaction he ripped it aside, tearing away buttons and fabric so he could cup her breast.

Magic.

Tessa sighed, the last of her rigid tension dissolving as even her bones seemed to liquefy.

If he could do this to her with the touch of one hand, the weighted caress of his palm, the not-so-gentle tweak of her nipple that made her whole body jolt in response…

Dimly Tessa realised she was passing the boundaries of previous experience.

And never had she wanted anything more than the heady sensations of him touching her, pleasing her.

His hand slipped around her back and she sighed as he yanked her bra undone, bending her arm to pull it aside. For then those long fingers were on her flesh, circling, squeezing, till the fire low in her body sent incendiary flares right through her and she thought nothing would ever quench the heat.

'More,' she breathed against his lips, as her own hands insinuated themselves between their locked bodies. She fumbled with his tie, then gave up, homing in on the precise line of buttons marching down his chest. He pulled back, just enough for her to work the buttons free.

He muttered something gruff in the back of his throat as she pushed her hands into the opening she'd made.

Bliss! His skin was hot, smooth, enticing with its fuzz of hair tickling her palms.

She wanted to feel it against her bare breasts.

He pulled her to him and her eyes closed at the dazzle of pleasure erupting within her. Her breasts against the solid masculine muscle of his chest. The heat and power and sheer erotic invitation as their bodies met. The teasing, stimulating feel of his body hair against her nipples.

She sucked in a breath, overcome by the barrage of feelings. Of desire.

Again his mouth took hers and now the urgency between them heightened to frantic. He leaned over, pressing her deep into the mattress, and she explored his bare skin beneath his open shirt. Her hands lingered on the powerful bulge of muscles she discovered, revelling in the sense of so much physical strength focused on her.

Stavros was busy with the fastening of her jeans, the zip, tugging the denim down her thighs just enough to slide his palm down and cover the feminine mound between her legs.

Tessa's body jolted as darts of pleasure arced out from his

touch to every part of her body. She stiffened, barely breathing, registering the feel of his long fingers against her.

Her gasp of pleasure was barely audible as he delved his tongue deeper into her mouth.

Restlessly she moved against his touch as it slid down to probe slowly, deeply.

'Oh…my—'

His mouth on hers stifled speech as Tessa spun out of control beneath his sexy body and his deliberately, unashamedly erotic exploration.

She tried to widen her legs, to allow him more access, but the jeans were tight around the tops of her thighs. That only heightened the urgency of her reaction, the burgeoning need to open herself to him.

Tessa's fingers dug into his shoulders as the darkness behind her closed eyelids whirled with impossibly bright shimmers of light. Her breath heaved, completely out of control, and she trembled in need, anticipation, desire.

Then his hand was gone, leaving her throbbingly eager and unsatisfied. Her eyes shot open as his lips left hers and she dragged in her first unfettered breath.

She tightened her grip on his shoulders, but he didn't seem to notice her restraining hands. His eyes, febrile and glittering, surveyed the jagged rise and fall of her bare breasts and then moved lower.

Tessa's lips throbbed from his assault. She wanted him back. Her breath sawed, loud in her throat. Arousal flooded her at the look in his eyes. His stillness lasted only a moment. Long enough for her to absorb the sight of him, taut and ready, and to want him.

He pushed himself away from her and off the bed, to kneel before her, yanking her jeans down, pulling off her sandals and tearing the last of her clothing away.

Tessa flushed, a burning rush of blood suffusing her whole

body as he stared down at her. She could feel the blush, and his hot gaze, all over her.

And it wasn't from embarrassment.

She wanted him so badly; had never known desire could be this raging beast inside.

She inched her thighs open a fraction and the moment of stillness ended. Stavros ripped open the knot of his tie and threw it away, stripped off the shirt down to the cuff-links, then unceremoniously tore those open, his shirt flying in pieces across the bed.

And as his hands lowered to the bulging fabric of his trousers he spoke. It was a low, guttural, uneven thread of Greek that made Tessa's skin draw tight.

She closed her eyes, trying to regain some semblance of control over her body.

She was aware of her heart's pulsing thud, hammering at her ribcage as if trying to escape, and the heat, the burning, feverish heat that consumed her. She heard him discard his clothes and the brief rustle of tearing foil.

Then suddenly there was more.

She cried out as he lowered his mouth to her, slid his tongue where his fingers had caressed her. Flames scorched and an inferno of white-hot sensations consumed her. It was pleasure so intense surely it must be pain.

'Please...Stavros!' Vaguely she caught the sound of the keening, breathless cry, unaware that she'd even called out. Every nerve, her whole being, concentrated on this indescribable pleasure.

Tessa was overcome by shuddering anticipation as he surged higher, over her trembling form, nuzzling at her skin. His body, all pure, muscled energy, and flaming hot, slid along her as he rose.

'Open your eyes,' he demanded in a gruff voice. 'I want you to see when I fill you.'

Obediently her eyes snapped open. She looked up to his face, drawn tight with barely constrained desire. She'd never seen anything so wonderful.

Then she felt something move against her and her gaze lowered, down over the bunched muscles and sinews of his chest and straining arms, over the taut abdomen to his arousal, sheathed in a condom. It was enormous, pushing rhythmically against her thigh.

Tessa swallowed, eyes rounding in apprehension, and yet of its own volition her body rose up towards his. Surely it would be all right, she told herself. This was how it was meant to be. This was…natural.

Stavros lowered his hand to her delicate flesh and instantly all anxiety vanished as the urgent wellspring of need surged inside her again.

She raised her eyes to his, opened her mouth to say his name, and instead gasped out a hoarse cry of pain as with a single, unstoppable thrust he filled her, surely to breaking point.

CHAPTER TEN

STAVROS shuddered, bracing himself on both arms above her as he sought to find a way back from the brink. The scent of her skin was such a powerful aphrodisiac that just breathing was an incitement to fulfilment.

He stilled, fighting down the compulsion to lose himself in the drugging ecstasy of sensation where her body cradled his. Her hot, sexy, impossibly tight, *inexperienced* body.

Hell!

Through the sensual fog that hazed his brain, he caught and absorbed that single thread of knowledge.

Why hadn't she told him? How was he supposed to have guessed the truth?

Her eyes were closed, shut tight in a frown of pain that said it all. But not as eloquently as the naked anguish he'd read in her wide, glazed eyes a moment ago as she'd stared up at him, like an injured animal, stunned by sudden trauma.

Stavros gritted his teeth, forcing himself to be still. No matter that he was on a knife's edge. A hair's breadth of movement would toss him over the precipice to a place where restraint shattered and the animal in him would be free to complete what he'd begun.

Her breath came in choppy little pants. Even that was

almost too much for him as his gaze dropped to her pert breasts rising and falling below him. He wanted to...

Another stifled gasp instantly stilled the automatic slide of his body against hers.

A virgin.

His wife was a virgin.

It didn't matter how many times he repeated the words in his mind, they still didn't make any sense.

If only he'd known he wouldn't have touched her.

Liar.

Even the knowledge of her innocence wouldn't have stopped him. She was a fever in his blood, had been since the beginning. With every day she stayed here it had become inevitable that this happened.

He hung his head, tension at breaking point across his shoulders as he fought for control. Taking his weight on one hand, he wrapped his other arm beneath her and rolled to his side, then to his back, keeping her clamped close.

Still they were intimately joined, but now Tessa was a warm, limp blanket above him and his hands smoothed over her bare back, as if somehow that might soothe the hurt he'd inflicted.

Held close in his arms, she felt like every male fantasy come to life, her naked flesh as soft and decadent as in any erotic dream. Her long hair spilling over him was that of a temptress. The innocence of her somehow was more exciting than anything he'd experienced.

He told himself he should be ashamed, finding primal, possessive satisfaction in the knowledge that he was her first, the only man she'd allowed in. Instead he gloried in the knowledge.

'I hurt you,' he said abruptly, his voice gruff. 'I'm sorry.' Never before had he needed to say that to a woman he'd taken to bed. To *any* woman.

She lifted her head and their eyes met. She looked stunned, pupils dilated and eyes overbright.

'I—' She cleared her throat. 'I'm OK.'

Sure. And he was Prince Charming. He hadn't missed the unsteadiness in her voice. Anyone could tell—

His eyes closed on a pang of pleasure as her muscles squeezed around him. Did she have any idea what that did to him? He stifled a groan.

There it was again. Tentative at first, then stronger, drawing him deeper, just where he most wanted to be.

Stavros opened his eyes and found her staring, those large, luminous eyes fixed on him. Her expression had changed. Her tempting lips were parted in a pout that resonated with sensual awareness.

She looked like a woman ready for a man. The realisation sent his blood pumping. Anticipation roared through him.

Now it would be all right.

Yet he'd need to be careful, take it slowly and let her set the pace. It would probably kill him. But at least he'd die smiling.

Tessa stared down at the broad chest beneath her, registered the sheen that glistened on his dark-gold flesh and wished she had the nerve to reach out and caress him as she itched to.

In that first, frightening moment when she'd absorbed the shock of his penetration, Tessa had feared that what she'd so longed for was a physical impossibility. That he was too big, she too small, for this to work. But as the seconds had lengthened and Stavros had let her adjust to the invasion of his body, the shock had worn off. The sting of pain had disappeared. Even the discomfort of this new experience had eased. Now she wanted…

She wanted…him.

Tentatively she hitched herself a little higher and immediately felt the convulsive tightening of his hands in the small of her back, pressing her close.

Oh, that felt good. Everywhere it felt good. She shut her eyes, focusing on these remarkable new sensations.

Was that a rumble of sound, deep in his chest? She opened her eyes and met Stavros' gaze. His lids were lowered, hooded at half-mast over sultry eyes that sent a tingle through her blood. She sighed and her chest moved against his, the friction delicious.

And then slowly, almost gently, he tilted his hips up against hers. The resulting sensation made her blood sing.

At her hiss of surprise he stopped and she could have cursed out loud. 'Please,' she murmured, lifting her head higher. 'Do that again.'

His gaze dropped to where her breasts met his bare flesh and heat shimmered in the air between them. Tessa felt it burn right through her.

His lips curved into a tight smile that made her wonder if he was in pain. Again, oh, so slowly, he pushed up and she trembled at the force of the reaction rippling through her.

'That's…' She swallowed down on her dry, scratchy throat. 'That's—'

'Good?' he murmured.

She shook her head. 'Good' didn't go anywhere near describing how wonderful it felt.

'Better than that,' she sighed as he moved again and automatically she tilted her hips to meet him. Her eyelids drifted lower at the heady bliss of this slow seduction.

'Sit up,' he urged, clasping her shoulders and pulling her higher till she sat astride him, her calves against his hips. 'That's it.' His voice died away in a drawn-out groan that echoed her sigh of satisfaction. Nothing had ever felt as good as this, especially when he rocked her slowly.

Then his hands were on her breasts, his mouth was there, and she shuddered at the overloading of exquisite sensations bombarding her body.

His tempo increased, as did her response. Their slow coupling lost its smoothness, grew faster, their movements urgent. His hands moved to her hips, clamping her hard in place against him. Still his tongue caressed her breast.

Tessa revelled in the magic that he spun for her and in the almost desperate way he held her to him, as if he had no intention of ever letting her go.

She didn't have time to process that thought before he leaned back on the bed, his gaze holding hers, and she was mesmerised anew by the potent need glittering in his eyes.

Warm air caressed her nipples, still wet from the lap of his tongue. Suddenly she didn't miss the caress of his mouth for a charge of energy shivered through her as he strove even higher against her.

She braced herself on his shoulders as the shiver grew to a trembling that spread right through her. Her body stiffened, awash with new delights, new pleasure. She welcomed the sense of being anchored against him by his touch and by the gaze that seemed to draw her to him, reassure and excite her at the same time.

Tessa opened her mouth to say something, she had no idea what, when out of nowhere a crescendo of escalating sensations shook her and the world tilted. Her fingers dug into his shoulders. She reached crisis point and waves of shuddering response racked her taut body. Waves of ecstasy. They rolled over her, through her, absorbing her, tossing her high. Only Stavros' hands, his gleaming eyes, kept her safe.

On and on it went, till the breath she'd held so long whooshed out of her lungs and she collapsed against him. Instantly strong arms wrapped round her, pulling her close even as the quivering aftershocks of her climax absorbed something new—the sensation of Stavros' body stiffening in spasm, of him shuddering, pulsing within her.

Her heart squeezed tight as she splayed her fingers over his silky, slick skin, a strange sense of protectiveness welling within her. Tessa wrapped her arms around his shoulders, as if she could hold him safe from the chaos that must surely underlie such bliss, just as he'd anchored her.

Finally, after an impossibly long time, the shuddering stopped. The only movement was his chest rising and falling beneath her and the thud of his heart like the slam of pistons.

Rough breathing filled the air.

Drowsily she was thankful that he didn't choose to say anything. For she wanted to hold on to the utter magic of this moment, of the incredible experience they'd shared, without harsh reality intervening.

She felt warm, limp, sated and utterly blissful.

Her last cogent thought was to register pleasure as Stavros shifted his hands away from her hips and up to wrap about her back, holding her close. She fell asleep to the gentle caress of his palm sliding in tiny, reassuring circles against her bare skin.

Tessa woke to a sensation of warmth. She snuggled closer, curiously replete and with a feeling of such contentment that she didn't want to wake. This was too nice. Too luxurious.

It was a moment before she registered the fact that it wasn't a soft pillow beneath her head, or a hard pallet. It was a solid cushion of pure muscle. Of warm skin. Short, silky hairs tickled her cheek, making her want to turn her head and nuzzle the masculine chest supporting her.

Stavros.

The knowledge breathed through her with the salt-musk aroma of his skin and something clenched deep inside her.

Tessa barely had time to absorb the fact, to realise that the warmth she felt was his embrace, holding her close in his bare arms, against his bare body, when he spoke.

'Wake up, Tessa.'

No! She didn't want to lose this wonderful floating sense of wellbeing. Even in her foggy state she understood that full awareness would bring the real world crashing in. She wanted to avoid reality just a little longer.

But then he spoke near her ear, his lips moving against her hair in a way that shot a twist of delight through her. 'Come on. Open your eyes.'

Reluctantly she lifted her lids, focusing on the sculpted male beauty of his chest just in front of her eyes and on the rounded muscles of his shoulder and biceps.

'That's it,' he murmured. Then he was moving, lowering her. She opened her mouth to protest but hissed in a shocked breath as warm water closed around her. Warm water, fresh-scented with a fragrance reminiscent of forests. A bath. A very deep bath.

The hiss transformed to a sigh as she registered the luxurious comfort of the water, like a sensuous, soothing tide about her. Aches she'd barely been awake enough to notice began to ease even as she leaned back. Slowly Stavros slid his arms away and Tessa bit her tongue against the urge to protest. She wanted him to hold her. She'd felt so secure in his arms.

Looking up, she found him watching her, his eyes sober.

He turned and strode over to yank open a cabinet, tug out a black silk dressing gown and shrug it over his naked body. The fabric pulled snugly around his shoulders and chest, lovingly outlining the curve of his musculature. If she were a different sort of woman she'd complain. Sexy as he looked in the sleek material, it couldn't compare with the perfection of his toned, golden body.

Their eyes met as he wrapped the belt around his lean waist and tied it tight. He stood, arms akimbo, with one dark eyebrow tilted in query.

Tessa felt the blush rise in her cheeks. But there was no way he could know what she was thinking.

'Why didn't you warn me?'

What? Dragging herself from the hypnotic spell he'd cast

over her, she sat up straighter, grateful now for the bubbles that kept all but her shoulders and head out of sight.

'You could have *told* me you were a virgin.'

His tone made her freeze, her heart thudding in her breast. He made it sound like an accusation. Something to be ashamed of. As if somehow her virginity had spoilt the experience for him.

She frowned, wondering if that could be it. True, she hadn't really known how to please him and had just let instinct guide her. But there'd been no doubting he'd climaxed every bit as spectacularly as she had.

'Did it really matter?' The words were out of her mouth before she'd even thought about them.

He stepped close, looking grim with his knitted brow and intense stare.

'It helps to know these things,' he said tightly.

'Oh.'

She watched his chest heave as he sighed, the sound heavy and deliberate. Like someone who didn't want to be having this conversation.

Well, that made two of them!

'If I'd known, I would have been more careful. I could have made it easier for you.'

He was worried that he'd hurt her? True, she still felt *odd*, but the sharp sting of pain was long gone. A bubble of pleasure welled inside her at the thought of his concern. Then reality intervened, obliterating the sweet fantasy that he genuinely cared.

'Would you have believed me if I'd told you? Like you listened when I said I'd been in South America all this time? Or when I promised I hadn't contacted the Press?'

She watched his features harden as he scrutinised her from his lofty height.

Oh, what was the use? Did she really expect an admission of guilt, or an apology? She closed her eyes, unable to face him any longer.

The truth was, she wanted neither from him.

Making love with Stavros had been the most profound experience of her life. Reaction shuddered through her as she realised the enormity of what she'd done, giving in to those urgent cravings. She didn't want an apology. Instead she longed for…what? His passion? His tenderness? *His love?*

She'd done the one thing common sense dictated she *not* do. She'd acted on impulse and fury and against her self-protective instincts. She'd made love to a man who saw her as an enemy. All because she'd fallen in love with a phantom, a man who'd never really existed. The man of her dreams, who was so similar and yet so different from Stavros Denakis.

The brush of soft fabric along her arm made her eyes pop open. There he was. Stavros. Leaning over the bath as he trailed a flannel over her shoulder and across her collar-bone. His features were still, unreadable, but the grimness had faded from his eyes and around his mouth.

Nevertheless, she wanted to be alone. Didn't he realise that? She felt far too vulnerable with him so close. The last thing she wanted was him touching her like that. Not now.

'Don't. I can wash myself.' She reached for the flannel but he tugged it away from her fingers.

Smoky grey eyes held hers for so long that eventually she felt her resolve and her indignation crumble. There was banked fire in his expression that reminded her vividly of what had just passed between them. A remembrance of the delight they'd shared. Heat flared in her cheeks. It had nothing to do with the warmth of the bath and everything to do with the shadow of desire she saw in his eyes.

His lips curled up in a tight, lop-sided smile that stole her breath.

'But it's so much more pleasant to have me do it for you. Isn't it?' His voice held an intimate, husky note that made her insides melt.

The cloth swiped down her arm and back up, grazing her hip and breast on the way. She sucked in a breath at the sheer sensual pleasure of it. The power he had over her, just from his touch, was incredible. So much for her indignation. Her will-power dissolved, overcome by her own yearning need.

'I...'

'Shh, Tessa. Just relax and let me bathe you.'

With a sigh of exhausted pleasure, she gave up and leaned back, closing her eyes.

Firmly Stavros kept his mind on the task at hand. Bathing Tessa. Soothing her hurts. *Not* focusing on her nude body laid out like an invitation to bliss before him, just visible through the thinning film of bubbles. *Not* on the way her breasts swayed as he slid the cloth across them, seductively brushing his hand as he stroked down her side.

Her eyes were shut but there was a frown on her face. From pain?

He'd slammed into her untried body with all the finesse of an over-sexed stallion. He'd shown the care, the sensitivity of a bulldozer.

He washed her hip. Her long, shapely thigh. Trying to ignore the more curvaceous shape of her still-slim body that a week of decent eating had produced.

Things had changed irrevocably. Inexperienced or not, Tessa had shown him a taste of sensual pleasure so extraordinary, so intense, he couldn't ignore it. No man could.

The die was cast.

He might have to call on every seductive skill he possessed but he intended to have her again. And again...and again.

Tessa opened her eyes when he finally pulled her out of the bath. While he concentrated on rubbing her dry with a plush towel she tried to read his mood.

The concentration on his face, the hint of a frown between his dark brows and the way his hair flopped down over his forehead as he bent to rub her legs dry made something in her want to reach out and hold him close. Whisper that she'd never felt like this about any other man.

Anticipation fizzed in her blood as he carried her to the big bed in his room. He put her down on the sheets and climbed in behind her, pulling the coverlet over them both. Her mouth dried and her heartbeat sped up.

Tessa knew she should leave. She should assert her independence and show some backbone, instead of holding her breath, waiting for his touch.

Sex with Stavros had been a mistake. Some tiny, still-functioning part of her mind knew it.

But what a glorious disaster!

And now, despite the urgings of her saner self, she stayed where she was. Ultimately she'd pay the price for succumbing to this man. Why not enjoy this moment of madness before it ended and reality flooded in?

His arms closed around her, pulling her tight against him. At her back Tessa felt the pulse of his heartbeat, his hot flesh, his arousal. Her breathing notched up as she remembered the sensations of their bodies together, moving, straining, climaxing.

Could it possibly be that wonderful a second time?

He lowered his lips to her ear and every nerve strained to attention. She held her breath.

'Shut your eyes, Tessa, and relax. Just go to sleep.'

CHAPTER ELEVEN

EARLY-MORNING light rimmed the curtains. She woke to lethargy, heat and a sense of restlessness. It was as if Stavros encompassed her. The rhythmic thud of his heart beat against her back. One solid thigh rested between hers, one large hand cupped her breast and his erection pressed tight against her buttocks. A zing of expectation caught her breath and she couldn't prevent the tiny involuntary wiggle of her body against his.

'You're awake.' The words feathered her ear and she closed her eyes in delight at the sensation of his breath caressing her bare skin.

'Yes.' She waited for him to tell her to leave. To fling some accusation at her.

'I'm sorry,' he murmured.

Sorry? Stavros was apologising? Her brain baulked at the unfamiliar concept even as a flicker of recollection told her he'd said something similar last night.

'I behaved without restraint. Like an animal.' There was no doubting his sincerity. Yet still he held her. His hardened body told its own tale.

Tessa tried to turn to see his face, but he was jammed so close she couldn't find the purchase to move. Besides, the feel of his hand at her breast sent heady thrills of delight through her and she didn't want to push him away.

'I rather enjoyed it,' she whispered.

Silence.

She sighed, not wanting to rehash it all. It was done now. For good or ill. She didn't have the stomach to fight him any more, or to dredge up accusations about how he'd never trusted her. As they lay, spooned together, it was almost as if all that had happened to two different people. People who'd existed in some distant past, long ago.

Before last night.

For now it was enough that he held her close in his arms.

Was she a fool for believing that the man she'd seen last night, bathing her hurts and denying the physical gratification he so obviously wanted again, was the *real* Stavros? The man with genuine tenderness in his touch, despite his grim visage?

Perhaps this was self-delusion to believe she'd broken through his implacably hard shell to discover the man she'd suspected was there all along. The man she'd glimpsed in South America: bold and decisive and selfless. Who worried about his sick father and treated the older man with just the right mix of respect and humour. Who'd been so protective of Angela.

A spear of pain lanced her at the memory of his ex-fiancée. Did he still love her?

'Even now I can hardly believe you were so inexperienced.'

Until last night. The unspoken words pulsed between them and his hand tightened a fraction at her breast, sending darts of shivery delight through her body.

She shrugged, her shoulder moving across his broad chest, reminding her of the hard-packed power surrounding her in his deceptively relaxed form. Excitement quickened her blood. How could she ever hope to win this uneven struggle against her own weakness?

'Abstinence has its own appeal sometimes.' Especially when the alternative had been rape at gunpoint. Tessa shivered at the memory of hair's-breadth escapes from militia fighters.

His hand slid from her breast as he wrapped his arm round her waist to hug her closer. She missed his gentle, almost absent-minded caress with an intensity that appalled her. But the feel of Stavros, so hot and hard, right up against her, was sheer delight.

Desire flared, a tingling, unsettling ache that curled in her abdomen and lower, making her squirm. One night with him had turned her into a wanton. She couldn't concentrate when her body was accelerating into overdrive.

'And now?' His deep voice was pure temptation as his lips grazed the skin below her ear. She sighed as a tremor of response rippled through her.

'Do you still prefer abstinence?' He pressed against her, his long length a delicious invitation to pleasure.

Again Tessa felt that melting sensation between her thighs. When he cupped her breast again she put her hand over his, feeling his fingers gently squeeze. She bit her lip so as not to cry out her delight.

'No. I'm not interested in abstinence at the moment.' Was that her voice? So throaty and explicitly inviting?

'That makes two of us.' Stavros slid his hand from her breast to her waist. Her belly. Still he arrowed lower.

Tessa's breath hitched on a sigh of pleasure.

This time Stavros did it right. Or at least better than last night.

He took his time caressing her body with his hands and his mouth, exploring every sleek centimetre of her till she was fully aroused and wanting and they were both on fire.

The sound of her sultry voice pleading for him to stop, then begging him not to stop, almost sent him over the edge. Combine that with the heady, unique scent of her, the most potent aphrodisiac on the planet, and it was a miracle he had any shred of control left.

Especially when she writhed beneath him, urging him

closer. Or when she reached out, her touch hesitant, almost awkward, yet like magic on his tortured flesh.

'Please, Stavros.'

He looked into her luminous emerald eyes and knew he couldn't resist any longer. Gently he lifted her legs as he settled over her, careful to brace himself so she could breathe. Her eyes were huge, her mouth a voluptuous pout of unwitting invitation. The feel of her soft skin against his was almost too much.

He paused, trying to marshal some restraint.

Tessa lifted her hands to his sides, then lower, palming his buttocks, and he surged forward, just enough to penetrate, and to wonder if there'd be pain this time.

Her eyes widened, her mouth sagged open as she breathed heavily. But there was no anxiety in her face.

Gingerly he moved, trying not to concentrate on the feel of her opening for him. Of her tightly embracing warmth welcoming him. Her fingers clamped hard, tugging him closer, and he went gladly, watching for signs of discomfort but finding none.

There was stillness as he tried to gather his wits and dredge up the control to take this slowly and make it right for her.

The trouble was, this felt like paradise. Like perfection. How could he resist it?

Asto kalo! No man could withstand the torture of this ultimate pleasure. Frantically he scoured his brain for something mind-numbing enough to distract him from the ecstasy of making love to Tessa. The opening of the new Denakis showrooms in Shanghai: that had enough problems to...

His breath hissed out as she moved against him. Automatically he responded so they rocked together.

Too soon, his mind warned, but then he felt it, the tell-tale stiffening of her hands on his flesh, the tremors that rippled through her like a swelling tide. Her breathing quickened and her eyes held his, her expression lost and wondering.

'It's all right, *glikia mou*,' he assured her. Then speech was impossible as the wildfire spread to his veins too and there was nothing but the pulsating throb of ecstasy as they rode the crest of fulfilment together.

It seemed a lifetime later that he lay stretched on his back, every muscle apparently dissolved in the conflagration that had melted all sense of self, all autonomy. He felt burnt clean by the inferno that had stripped him to the bone and to raw, visceral emotions.

The intensity of the experience stunned him.

He looked at the woman resting against him, her head on his chest, her long dark tresses spread over him. Her hand curled near his navel. One soft thigh rested over his, and at his side was the damp heat of her feminine centre.

She was a conundrum. An enigma. As unstinting in her responses and as sensuous as any man could wish. That must be why he wanted her so badly. Again. Already. Inevitably.

And yet she was innocent, sexually at least. All she knew was what he'd taught her.

Something like pride and pleasure inflated in his chest at the idea. Something that a civilised man wouldn't admit to. Nevertheless his lips curved up into a smile as he savoured that knowledge.

And she hadn't taken his money. In fact she'd signed it away. To what purpose? That niggled at him. How could he control this situation if he didn't understand it?

Just because she'd been a virgin didn't mean she wasn't after his money. Why else come straight here from South America? Her arrival during his betrothal party had been impeccably timed for maximum disruptive effect.

If she'd been as innocent as she claimed Tessa Marlowe would be in Australia right now, taking up her old life.

Stavros stroked his palm possessively down her back, noting with pleasure the instinctive way she responded to the caress, pressing her breasts forward, against him. She must be coming out of her light doze to react like that. Instantly the heat of anticipation prickled his skin.

He still had to find out what she was up to and why she'd indulged in the defiant gesture with the contract. But there was time to pursue that. And other things.

His hand swept the curve of her hip and back up. He smiled. An annulment was out of the question now. At least on the grounds of non-consummation.

So it would have to be a divorce. It might take longer, but that was no problem. In fact, it would be a pleasure. *His pleasure.*

He intended to make the most of this time with his uninvited spouse. By the time the legalities were completed he'd have her measure, his curiosity would be satisfied and this passion would have burned out.

Stavros deliberately ignored the proprietary thoughts Tessa aroused in him. Those were his hormones speaking. It couldn't be anything else. He knew only too well that romantic love was an illusion. Hadn't he watched his father fall victim to that particular dream time and again?

These possessive stirrings in his blood were entirely natural, especially given the fact that he was Tessa's first lover.

They didn't mean anything more.

CHAPTER TWELVE

In the days since she and Stavros had fought and ended up in his bed, so much had changed. Gone was the cold, hard-as-nails tormentor and in his place was a man who seemed intent on turning Tessa's most secret fantasies into reality.

That first day he hadn't left her side. They'd barely left his bed. Even now the memory of his passion, his vigour and his tenderness brought a flush to her cheeks. When he channelled that formidable energy into the task of pleasing a woman the results were mind-boggling.

After that he'd only gone to Athens for quick trips in the afternoons while Tessa slept. She needed the time to recuperate from the long nights that stretched well into daylight, when their mutual desire was unquenchable.

It was bliss. Better than anything she'd imagined.

And it can't last, she told her reflection in the bathroom mirror.

She was living in a fool's paradise, giving in to what she felt for Stavros, succumbing to his passion, his intensity, his voracious sexuality. To his beguiling, heart-stopping tenderness. To the illusion that fantasy had become real.

This was no life for her, living in limbo with neither a commitment given nor any discussion of emotional ties.

She *knew* it. In the few waking moments when he was away

from her side, the knowledge tortured her. But for once she wanted to live the dream, to grab life by the throat and *enjoy* it. Not worry about the future, or the past. Surely after the last few years she was entitled to just a taste of her favourite fantasy: she and Stavros together, inseparable. In love.

Surely the damage was already done, now she'd given herself to him. Leaving immediately would be just as hard as leaving in a few days or weeks. Why not enjoy the exquisite delights of being his lover, store up memories of bliss against the time she'd be alone again?

Nothing was more certain than that she'd be alone again one day. She'd never really belonged anywhere, had always been the outsider. She should be used to it by now, able to cope when the time came to leave.

Yet she refused to give in to self-pity. Her head held high, she pulled open the door and walked through to the bedroom.

As always, Stavros captured her attention immediately. He stood near the door, wearing chinos and a black short-sleeved shirt that revealed his strong, sinewy forearms.

Just as inevitably his slow smile of welcome heated her blood to instant boiling point.

How could she even *consider* leaving him?

It wasn't until he motioned her closer that she noticed the long rack of clothes inside the bedroom door.

'For you, Tessa,' he murmured, gesturing her forward.

'For me?' She frowned, slowly crossing the room to stop in front of the row of hangers.

'Of course, for you.' He sounded lazily indulgent.

'But why?' Her mouth gaped as she took in the array of rich colours, the delicate fabrics, the scent of wealth.

'You need something to wear.' His baritone sounded from just behind her and his arms came round to clasp her loosely against him. As usual she melted straight into his embrace, glorying in the support of his strong frame.

Somehow, one day soon, she'd have to drum up the strength to resist him and move back to the real world. She shut her eyes as he rubbed his cheek against her unbound hair, a gesture she'd come to love in these last days. An affectionate gesture, as if he reciprocated her feelings.

'But I don't need that many.' To her bewildered eyes there were enough outfits to clothe a whole village several times over.

His hand inched up to circle her breast and his breath feathered, hot and arousing, on the side of her neck. 'If I had my way, you wouldn't need any at all.' His lips slid along her skin and she shivered. Already her body was softening, muscles loosening, blood pumping faster in anticipation.

It would be so easy to succumb to the dictates of her body, to the invitation in his rumbling whisper, and turn in his arms, kiss him and let the world spin away.

Too easy.

Without consciously deciding to, she pulled away, stepping out of his embrace and towards the collection of clothes. The air seemed cool on her arms after Stavros' embrace and she slid her hands up and down them.

Hesitantly she reached out and touched a dress as soft and light as gossamer. Then another, of some slinky fabric that spilled through her hand like liquid. These weren't *her* sort of clothes. She was a cotton and denim girl. She'd never even looked at clothes like these before.

'I can't wear these.' She slid her hands from one gorgeous outfit to the next. Dresses, jackets, trousers, skirts of swirling silk. She shook her head, amazed that he'd even suggested it.

She wouldn't have objected to a cotton skirt and top, a new pair of jeans. But in these she'd look like someone pretending to be what they weren't.

'This is too much.'

'Why?' He stood close; she could sense his presence from the way her neck tickled. 'Why is it too much?'

If he didn't know that, he didn't understand women's fashion. That she couldn't believe. Not when his company made some of the finest jewellery ever to adorn a beautiful woman. She'd seen the photos in the guest suite's expensive magazines and they'd taken her breath away.

'I couldn't wear these. I'd look…' She shrugged, not wanting to try describing how ridiculous she'd look in designer outfits. 'Just something casual is what I need.'

'They *are* casual,' he murmured and again the timbre of his voice sent awareness spreading through every nerve.

'*This* is casual?' She pulled out a dress of emerald green, of some silky fabric that must have cost the earth.

Beside her his arm reached out so he could stroke the whisper-soft material. Her stomach knotted at the sight of his large, broad hand splayed over the bodice, the waist, the flaring skirt. She watched the movement and it was as if he stroked *her.* She could almost feel the brush of his fingers over her skin: slow, deliberate and sensuous. Her throat closed in a convulsive movement.

'Perhaps not this one,' he agreed. 'But I can see you wearing it. You'll look gorgeous.'

Tessa eyed the dipping neckline, the pure decadence of the gorgeous, sexy dress and knew she'd never carry it off. It was designed for an altogether different sort of woman. Not someone ordinary like her.

She put the hanger back. 'It's not me,' she said firmly, even as her eyes lingered on the dress. She'd never seen anything so beautiful. The idea that Stavros wanted to buy it for her… If she weren't careful she'd convince herself that meant something other than that he was mega-wealthy and sick of seeing her tatty clothes. She might even persuade herself he wanted to buy her something pretty just for the pleasure of giving her a treat.

* * *

Stavros watched as she rifled through the hangers, looking for something to replace the ancient rags that were apparently all the clothes she owned.

She wouldn't find anything like them. This was all the finest quality, as befitted his lover. He didn't settle for second best and nor would she while she was with him.

She'd find him more than generous, with his time and his wallet. This relationship might be short, and unusual, since Tessa was technically his wife, but he always treated his women well. It was only if they tried to manipulate him, to barter sham affection for cash, that he objected.

He had no problem with honest lust and, for all her previous schemes, Tessa couldn't hide that. Her passion was genuine, every bit as real as the desire he felt for her. She didn't have the artifice to hide that, at least.

Besides, he *wanted* to see her dressed beautifully. His mouth had watered as soon as he'd seen the green silk dress, imagining Tessa wearing it for him. Its cut demanded a lithe, perfect body, which she had, and an almost total absence of underwear. *That* he could imagine only too well.

Heat flared under his skin as he pictured himself standing behind her, stroking his palms down the sensuous silk of that bodice, over her proud, ripe breasts, across her flat stomach, and lower, bunching the fabric in his hands higher and higher until…

'Stavros?' She'd turned towards him and was frowning. Obviously she'd been trying to get his attention.

In one hand she held a black one-piece swimsuit. 'I'll try this on. The others wouldn't suit me.'

He flicked a glance at the array of bright, minuscule bikinis she hadn't touched. His lips twitched and he repressed the urge to smile. One thing he'd learned about Tessa Marlowe was that, for all her delightful physical responsiveness, her natural sensuality, once out of bed she was deliciously shy about revealing her delectable body.

It was a challenge he looked forward to, persuading her to dress to please him, rather than to cover up.

She was naïve if she thought that little black number was anything like demure. He cast a connoisseur's eye over the scrap of Lycra, cut high at the hip and deceptively plain. It would fit her like a second skin, enhancing her delicate femininity.

'Put it on,' he said, 'and we'll swim. *But* when we come back you'll choose some other clothes as well. Or I'll choose them for you.'

'But—'

'No arguments, Tessa. I've been patient about this long enough. If you don't do it willingly I'll have those rags you currently own burned. Then what would you wear?'

Her eyes widened in astonishment. He paced slowly towards her, stifling a grin as she automatically backed away from him. Heat sizzled through his bloodstream at the thought of making good his threat.

'You know *I* won't mind at all if you live here completely naked.' He almost wished she'd continue to fight him on this. There'd be definite benefits.

'All right,' she murmured at last, capitulating as he knew she would. 'I'll find something else later.' With one swift glance at him, she ducked her head and hurried into the bathroom to change.

Stavros turned to the house phone. The pool was in a private courtyard, but still…

'Security?' he said, watching the *en-suite* door close behind Tessa. 'I want complete privacy this afternoon. No one is to go near the pool yard. Understood?'

Stavros smiled as he severed the connection. There were definite benefits to having his current lover living in his home. He intended to take full advantage of every one.

* * *

Stavros took the stairs two at a time, eager to see if Tessa was waiting for him in the bedroom. All the way back from his meeting in Athens he'd been unable to concentrate on business. Even the final arrangements for the Shanghai showrooms had failed to hold his attention because he was fantasising about her. Waiting for him. Naked.

Naked, or maybe in one of the sexy, barely there negligées he'd bought her. A surge of heat filled him as he walked towards the bedroom.

He pushed open the door. Empty. Putting his laptop down, he strode to the bathroom to make sure she wasn't there, a slick, perfumed water nymph awaiting his pleasure.

No sign of her.

He grinned ruefully as he yanked off his tie and slipped his jacket from his shoulders. He needed to have a word with Tessa about how best to please an impatient lover.

He'd never yet found her here waiting for him. Instead she'd been in the kitchen, making pastries under his housekeeper's approving eye, or swimming, or even helping his reluctant groundsman in the kitchen garden!

Yet Stavros had no complaints. Her response when she looked up and saw him was always the same: that sweet smile of welcome, the passionate kiss of surrender that never failed to make his body harden and his breath seize.

No business coup had ever been as satisfying as initiating Tessa into the delights of sex. Even the piquancy of knowing he was her first and only lover was eclipsed by the ever-present passion between them.

No lover had ever been so unstinting in her passion.

No one had ever made him feel so…happy.

He dropped his cuff-links in a drawer and went in search of her, rolling up his sleeves as he went.

Nearing the stairs, he caught the rich scent of orchids and paused. He glanced at the floral display on a nearby table. The fragile, spectacularly beautiful blooms instantly reminded him of Tessa. He reached out and touched a petal, soft as velvet. Just like her skin, especially the spot behind her ear. That sensitive place where just the graze of his teeth could send her wild.

He smiled. He'd never really noticed the flowers in his home before. But there was a sensuality about these, a seductive, exotic quality that triggered thoughts of Tessa, his exquisite, intriguing conundrum.

For even after weeks of fantastic sex and, to his surprise, of genuine companionship, she was still a puzzle. A secret that lay just beyond his understanding.

He loped down the stairs and headed for the kitchen.

He knew much more about her character now, but not enough. He *knew* she didn't fake her responses to him, *knew* she enjoyed being with him, *knew* that she even, for reasons that escaped him, had a soft spot for his father.

His employees liked her too. In his experience that was telling. His stepmothers had, to a woman, been abrupt and dismissive with the staff. Nor had she tried to milk him for expensive trinkets. She'd only accepted a few paltry clothes. How did that fit with the money-hungry woman who'd raced round the globe to extort money?

He tried to match the clever, avaricious schemer with the woman of simple tastes. The woman who'd flowered before his eyes with just a little care and attention.

Then finally it struck him.

Unlike that of so many women he'd known, and even bedded, her aim wasn't a lifestyle of conspicuous consumption. Instead she wanted simple financial security. That had to be it.

Given her unsettled childhood, the lack of funds that she'd skated over when describing her youth, the low-paying jobs, her time in South America, was it any wonder?

He remembered the horror on her face when she'd thrown

his settlement offer in his face. Because she hadn't realised quite how enormously wealthy he was?

Or was he kidding himself? He paused, frowning, just outside the kitchen. Was she simply angling for more?

Yet every instinct told him she was genuine.

He pulled the door open and stepped forward. Then stopped in his tracks.

He'd found Tessa. And she wasn't alone.

Automatically he moved further into the room as the door swung shut behind him, bumping his hip. But his eyes remained fixed on her.

She'd never looked more beautiful. She was wearing the plainest of the outfits he'd bought her: light fitted trousers that showed off her trim figure to perfection and a top that almost matched the bright gleam of her eyes.

It wasn't her clothes that grabbed his attention, it was the sheer joy that radiated from her.

The impact of it warmed him where he stood.

In her arms she held a toddler. Stavros recognised him as his housekeeper Melina's grandson. The child was gurgling with laughter, trying to grab a brightly coloured ball from Tessa's hand. When he couldn't catch it he reached out and instead grasped a lock of her midnight silk hair that had escaped her pony-tail.

'Ow! Adoni, that's not fair.' But there was no real censure in her indulgent tone.

At the sight of her, face flushed, eyes brimming with laughter, something slammed into Stavros' chest and lodged here, immovable.

Was it the way she smiled at the child, as if nothing in the whole world was more important than him? Or was it the prospect of Tessa playing with her own baby, a few years from now? With a child given to her by another man.

A strange, achy sensation twisted inside him. A shudder

rippled through him and he planted his feet wider against its impact.

The force of what he felt rocked him, drawing his brows together in a frown. Yet he refused to analyse these disturbing feelings. To define what they meant. He worked on logic only, never on emotions.

'Stavros!' The sound of her breathless voice drew his attention. Good. This hollow sensation in his chest was no doubt something best ignored.

'I see I have a rival.' He forced a smile, only too glad to concentrate on his lover rather than on indefinable, unsettling emotions.

Tessa hugged Adoni closer in her arms as the impact of Stavros' smile hit her full-force. As always she felt it like a physical caress, one that rippled right through her, even making her toes curl. This time she felt relief too.

When she'd looked up and seen him there, a dark scowl on his brow and tension stiffening his shoulders, her heart had sunk. She'd wondered if something had happened to drag them back to the old days of distrust and accusation.

'Well, he *is* very handsome. Aren't you, Adoni?' She turned to the little boy and gave him the ball, knowing full well he didn't understand a word of English. He was only just starting to babble in Greek, according to his proud grandmother.

'You don't mind?' she asked, looking up at Stavros, still wondering about the frown she'd seen a moment before.

'Mind that I find you embracing another male in my absence?' He took a long stride closer, his expression mock-stern.

She shrugged. The Stavros she knew was no snob, but there must have been some reason for that black look of disapproval. 'I meant, me playing with Melina's grandson. I know that in some houses there's a demarcation line between staff and...guests.'

Guests must surely include her, she thought on a twinge of bitterness. How else would you classify a wife who was really no more than a mistress?

His eyebrows rose in surprise. 'Have you seen evidence of that here?'

Tessa shook her head. On the contrary, she'd met quite a few of the staff and they spoke of Stavros respectfully but affectionately, as if he were family.

'No. No, I haven't.'

'That's as it should be. They are all my people.'

She tilted her head in query. His people?

'From this island,' he explained. 'I have a policy of employing islanders here, and where possible in Denakis Enterprises. It's a way to support the local economy. Besides,' his smile flashed, 'they are the salt of the earth, these people.'

And clearly they thought the same way about him. Tessa had heard such praise. How he'd offered Melina her post as housekeeper when she'd been newly widowed and struggling to support her teenage children. How he funded small business loans for locals as well as scholarships for those who wanted to study on the mainland.

Originally she'd seen Stavros only as a mega-wealthy man but had never given thought to what he actually *did* with his money. It made her proud to know he was interested in other people and his community, not just in adding to his wealth.

Adoni wriggled in her arms, clearly tired of being held so long.

She looked up at Stavros, so close, so attractive, and felt that familiar tug of need deep inside.

'I'd better take Adoni back to his grandmother.'

Stavros' mouth curved in a knowing smile and his gaze heated as he met her eyes over the toddler's head.

'Don't be long, *glikia mou.*' His voice dropped on the endearment, transfixing her. 'I have plans for this evening.'

No doubting what he had in mind. And no doubting either that she'd be a more than willing participant. Where Stavros was concerned, she had no will-power left.

With a quick nod and a shaky smile, Tessa turned and headed for the back door. Melina was picking herbs for the evening meal. She'd take Adoni to her and then return to Stavros. Excitement squeezed her stomach at the thought.

Stavros watched her walk away. The gentle sway of her hips, the protective curve of her arms as she held the child, the seductive swing of her long hair across her back. Need tightened to a hard knot in his belly.

What was he going to do with her?

The sex was terrific. But more than that he *enjoyed* having Tessa here. He'd been delegating his work so he had more time with her. It was indulgent, out of character. And so satisfying.

He speared his fingers through his hair, searching for answers. Then, out of the blue, it hit him.

The hairs stood up on the back of his neck as an idea lodged in his brain.

Unorthodox. Unexpected. Unlikely.

Perfect.

He strode to the window to stand, watching her talk with Melina. And all the time he was busy, assessing the notion from every angle, possibilities and permutations clicking through his brain at lightning speed.

His father was lonely and wanted companionship.

Stavros wanted a family. Partly for the old man's sake, so he could see the next generation of Denakis sons. Partly because Stavros had come to realise he wanted more from life than could be gained from a balance sheet or the adrenaline rush of a tricky corporate negotiation.

Stavros wanted a wife. A sexy, intelligent woman who'd bear his children, make his home comfortable and offer the solace a man wanted after a long day.

And Tessa wanted security. Financial security, and, unless he'd missed his guess, the stability that came from having a family, permanence and belonging. One look at her holding Adoni told him all he needed to know about her views on children. She'd make a wonderful mother. Warm and caring.

He could see her now with their children. The mere thought of it made the blood pump faster through his body.

It was a perfect fit. *Tessa* was a perfect fit for his life and he could give her precisely what she wanted.

He ignored the urgent voice reminding him that Tessa was perfect in all sorts of much more personal ways.

And they were already married. No need for delay. No requirement for long negotiations or for tedious courtship.

His pulse quickened. No need for contraception. He guessed she'd be eager to try for a family. The thought of making long, slow, heart-pounding love to her, with no barrier between them, sent the blood pooling low in his body.

Instinctively he knew his decision was right. Not just right—it was perfect.

He'd cancel the divorce.

Instead he'd make Tessa an offer she couldn't refuse. A place here. As his wife.

CHAPTER THIRTEEN

WAS she a fool?

Tessa stared into the massive bathroom mirror, wondering if she'd lost her mind or whether, for the first time in her life, reality *was* better than her dreams.

Was she right to fight for what she wanted, despite the enormous odds against her?

Logic told her this was a big mistake. She should have confronted Stavros weeks ago about where he thought their relationship might lead. For despite his attentiveness, his concern for her wellbeing, his tender amusement and his unquenchable passion, he never spoke about the future.

Surely this was merely a short-term affair, fun and convenient for him. Something different from his usual liaisons with women of his own set.

Yet in her heart Tessa clung to the belief that there might be more to it. That in time he might realise how truly wonderful they were together.

Surely only a fool would hold out that hope.

Or a woman in love.

She stared into the overbright green eyes in the mirror before her, unblinking. Facing the truth.

That was why she'd stayed. Why she'd gambled her self-respect and pride and emotional security by remaining in Greece. Because she'd fallen in love with Stavros Denakis.

He embodied every quality she'd dreamed of in a partner, husband and lover: strength, caring, integrity and so much more besides. The idea of being without him was a cold, hard knot of dread in her stomach.

Yet she shied away from anything that might prompt him to discuss the future. She'd clung to the here and now with a desperation that barely concealed her fear of rejection.

Tessa squared her shoulders and lifted her chin. She'd come this far. She'd see it through. She owed it to herself to fight for her future.

Her gaze dipped to the reflection of her shoulders, almost bare in this dress, to the neckline that plunged between her breasts. The cut of the bodice meant she couldn't wear a bra and the sensation of the slinky fabric against her skin made her aware of her body in a way that was completely new. The fact that she wore only the tiniest wisp of sheer lace as underpants only heightened the excitement that hummed through her body.

Stavros had wanted to see her in this green dress. Despite her initial alarm at how much flesh the outfit revealed, now she was grateful. She knew the effect it would have on him. His libido was strong and constant. So perhaps he wouldn't notice her nervousness when she appeared in a designer dress, her fear that instead of a sexy, confident woman she'd look like a sparrow masquerading as a swan.

Maybe if she could carry this off then Stavros might look at her and see…what? A woman who wouldn't look out of place among his jet-set friends? A woman who could hold her own in sophisticated company?

She doubted it. But perhaps, just perhaps it might open his eyes to possibilities he hadn't considered.

Like staying married to his inconvenient wife.

She turned and pushed open the door, entering the bedroom

with the slow, hip-swaying walk imposed by the high-heeled satin evening shoes that went with the dress. Across the room Stavros looked up as he closed his laptop. Eyes like burning ice held hers. Her pace slowed, faltered, as her heart beat out of rhythm then accelerated, thumping hard and urgent against her rib-cage.

'Turn around.' His voice skated across her bare flesh like warm satin, and she flushed as she stopped and pivoted on one foot. Around her hips and thighs the dress flared and shifted, a caress against her skin.

His gaze trawled down her almost-naked back. In her heightened state of awareness Tessa could swear she felt it slide centimetre by centimetre down her spine. She shivered, imagining him tracing that line, arousing her with the touch of his lips.

When she turned to face him again he'd stepped closer. His eyes had darkened to blazing charcoal brightness. Her nipples tightened and pebbled as his gaze swept over her and she read the wanting in his taut features.

In this, at least, she had power.

'You are beautiful, *glikia mou*. Exquisite.' He stepped forward and took her hand in his, lifting it and pressing a kiss to the back of it. To her palm, her wrist.

Tessa shuddered as need pierced her. He only had to touch her, look at her that way, speak in that glorious, deep masculine voice and she was ensnared all over again.

In that moment she realised the devastating truth.

Even if he didn't envisage a long-term commitment between them, she'd stay and take whatever he chose to give of himself. She loved him that much.

'Come,' he murmured, pulling her close and tucking her hand into the curve of his elbow. 'Melina has promised us a special meal tonight.' His fingers laced through hers, gently caressing. 'We'd better go down. Otherwise I'll be sorely tempted to forget about food and persuade you to spend the whole evening here.'

He lifted his hand to the curve of her cheek, feathering across to her jaw and the pulse beating out of control there. He dipped his head to whisper in her ear. 'That dress deserves to be worn for at least half an hour before I take it off you.'

Tessa's tongue cleaved to the roof of her mouth as she envisaged him stripping the fabric away with those large, powerful hands. But she made herself smile up at him and shrug, aware of the way her breast pressed against his arm.

'We can't disappoint Melina. She's been cooking all afternoon.'

It was a perfect meal. Delicate savoury pastries that melted in the mouth. The freshest, most succulent seafood, prepared simply, to reveal its flavour. Chicken cooked in champagne. Tiny bread rolls that Melina had twisted into knots. Crisp vegetables. An array of local specialities that made Tessa wish she could do justice to the feast.

And the setting was pure fantasy. They ate in a secluded arbour right on the waterfront, lit by myriad tiny globes threaded through the climbing roses that surrounded them. In the distance the bobbing lamps on a passing boat decorated the velvety darkness.

A soft breeze made the candles on the table flicker, throwing shadows onto Stavros' face, accentuating the strong, masculine cast of his features.

Her heart felt full just looking at him. But she had no time to swoon over him, for Stavros, as usual, was intent on engaging her in animated discussion. Probing, debating and finding common ground on all sorts of subjects.

It was only as his gaze dipped repeatedly to the shadow of her cleavage that she realised he was having as much difficulty as she, ignoring the awareness that throbbed between them.

'I have something for you,' he said when the plates had been cleared away. His voice took on a sombre tone and instantly Tessa stiffened, wary of what might be coming. Was it another of his legal documents, limiting her claim on his precious money?

He reached into his pocket and drew out something dark and flat. Too small for papers. Tessa's breath caught as he put it down before her. Black velvet, decorated with a single gold triangle, the Greek letter delta. D for Denakis. She'd seen that symbol recently on the glossy pages of magazines that featured fabulous jewellery.

'For me?' Her voice shook. It was one thing for him to give her clothes when she had only threadbare hand-me-downs. It was another thing totally to offer her jewellery.

'For you.' He sat back, watching her. 'Open it.'

Tessa's mouth dried. This felt…momentous. Her mind whirred with the possibilities of what this gesture meant. Her hand was unsteady as she lifted the lid.

Emerald fire caught the light, dazzlingly bright. Tessa gasped. She'd never seen anything so beautiful. Her hand hovered over the large, square-cut gem in its simple antique-gold setting. But she didn't touch. She didn't dare. This had to be some mistake.

'It will look perfect on you.' His words were a low, throaty burr that made her skin prickle.

She stared at the exquisite pendant, unable to believe her eyes, or her ears.

'You're giving this to *me*?'

'It could have been made for you.' His voice slid like warm honey along her jangling nerves. 'But it's actually a family piece. It was worn by my mother and, before her, my grandmother.'

Tessa's lungs squeezed tight, cutting off the flow of air. There was a buzzing in her ears as she struggled to take it in. Stavros wanted to give her his *mother's* necklace? A gorgeous heirloom piece that looked as if it belonged on display in a museum? A piece that must surely hold incredible personal significance for him?

Her mind reeled at the implications. Could it be? Had Stavros fallen in love with her as she had him? Surely it was impossible, too soon after Angela. Yet hope burgeoned, strong and vibrant, in her heart.

Her gaze darted across to meet his, but he was already standing, moving around the table to lean over and scoop the glittering pendant from its nest of pure white satin.

Tessa held her breath as he stood behind her, and then lowered the necklace. She felt its weight on her bare skin, the touch of his hands, firm and warm, at her nape.

She didn't need a mirror to see if the pendant looked beautiful. Tessa *felt* beautiful, as she never had before. Her blood fizzed with the knowledge that Stavros cared for her enough to entrust her with something so precious to him. She didn't try to hide the radiant smile of joy that filled her face.

For now she knew.

Stavros loved her. He reciprocated the feelings she'd hardly dared dwell on, the emotions that made him the most important thing in her world.

It seemed a lifetime ago that she'd railed at the hard, deliberately brutal man who'd hurled accusations at her. Since then she'd discovered the side he kept private from the world: the tender, caring man, strongly protective, with a wicked, teasing sense of humour and unbounded passion. The man she loved with all her heart. Tears glazed her eyes and she blinked them back.

'I was right.' His voice was husky as he looked down from his immense height. 'It's perfect for you.'

His eyes were shadowed but Tessa read the stillness in his big frame and knew he felt it too, the momentousness of the occasion. She reached up a hand to the pendant and touched its hard facets, trying to ground herself in reality. Her heart pounded in her chest and her breasts seemed to swell as he looked down at her.

'Stavros, I...' What could she say that would convey the wealth of feelings inside her? There was only one answer: the obvious, the most important. *I love you.*

'Tessa,' he spoke before she got the words out, 'I've been thinking about us.'

He pulled his chair around the table to sit with her, knee-to-knee, drawing her hand into his. It was warm, solid and comforting and she never wanted to break its grip. Her words dried up as she watched him, willed him to say it, admit his feelings. She could hardly believe it was true, despite the unconscious signals these past weeks that had seemed to reveal a true tenderness for her.

'Yes?' Her voice was a breathless whisper.

His thumb stroked her wrist, teasing the pulse point, firming across her palm to locate the erogenous zone at its centre and send shivers of delight spreading out from there.

'This marriage of ours.' He paused for so long she wondered if he was groping for the right words. But that was impossible. Stavros was always so confident and articulate.

His lips firmed for an instant before he continued. 'I want to make it permanent.' His eyes held hers, his gaze intense and captivating. She couldn't look away, even though her stomach had gone into free-fall and her limbs had started to tremble.

'You want us to stay married?' She had to be absolutely sure she wasn't deluding herself.

'That's right.' His fingers tightened around her hand. 'I've already cancelled the divorce proceedings. I want you to be my wife. Permanently.'

The words echoed in her brain, dying away only gradually. Joy was a rising tide inside her, bubbling and bursting to be free.

But his face was so still, so sombre, with the light emphasising the almost grim cast of his features. Nor did he move to embrace her or kiss her.

Out of nowhere a single, ice-sharp splinter of doubt froze her, even as she opened her mouth to blurt out instant agreement.

His razor-edged gaze dropped to her mouth, then back to her eyes. It was only then that Tessa noticed how unreadable it was. No heat, no passion. *No love.*

He looked like a man intent on closing a business deal, poker-faced and wary. Giving nothing away.

'Why?' The word emerged as an almost silent croak and she tried again. 'Why do you want us to stay married?'

He didn't hesitate for an instant. 'It's the logical thing to do. Believe me, I've considered every angle and it works best for everyone.'

'Everyone?' Tessa's lips felt stiff and numb, as if with cold.

'That's right.' Once more his thumb stroked across her palm, but this time there was no shiver of erotic response, no quickening in her blood. Her body felt lifeless against his touch.

'We'll all gain by it. You most of all.' He paused as if waiting for her to say something. But she couldn't think what. Her brain had atrophied, trying to cope with the dawning revelation that Stavros saw their marriage as a matter of logic, not love.

'You'll belong here, as part of my family. You'll want for nothing. As my wife you'll have security, wealth, anything that an indulgent husband and a private fortune can provide.' Again he paused, but continued when her lips remained pressed together. 'We can start a family soon too. You want children, don't you?'

Tessa nodded. She'd always loved children. She'd dreamed of having some of her own when she found the right man. A man who loved her as she did him.

A sob rose in her throat and she choked it back. If she gave in to the welling pain that filled her, she was afraid she mightn't know how to stop.

Her hopes for love, her stupid dream that Stavros genuinely cared, were turning into a nightmare of epic proportions. If it didn't hurt so much it might even have been funny, the way she'd built herself up for such a fall. *Him,* wealthy, experienced and hard-edged, falling for ordinary Tessa Marlowe. Tessa, who'd never really belonged anywhere, and especially not here in a tycoon's mansion.

But it hurt so much just breathing against the stabbing pain that even a bitter grimace was impossible.

'Good,' he said with a taut smile of satisfaction. 'Then we can try for a family straight away.'

His voice seemed to come from a long way off and Tessa frowned. Had she heard him right? She swiped her tongue over her dry lips and swallowed down the burning lump of hurt in her throat.

'You want me to have your babies?'

'They will be beautiful babies, *glikia mou,* if they take after their mother. Can you visualise them, our son, our daughter?'

She must be imagining the emotion reverberating in his deep voice. She was knocked off balance by the appalling clarity with which she could indeed see their children in her mind's eye: playing here at the villa, learning to swim in the pool or down on the shore. Small, sturdy boys with their father's eyes and firm chin. A tiny daughter who could wrap her dad around her little finger.

It's not fair! Tessa wanted to wail out loud, thrash and hit out against his hold, rage against a cruel fate that offered her this travesty of what she most desired. The trappings of the life she'd dreamed of. Trappings that would only torture her with the knowledge that she didn't have the one thing that meant everything: Stavros' love.

Tessa pulled her hands from his grip and smoothed them up her arms, trying to warm herself against the chill that seeped out from her bones.

'It's time I had children, to carry on the Denakis name. It will please my father, who's desperate to see another generation. But I want a family as well, Tessa. It's time for me to settle down with one woman.'

He leaned close, trailing his knuckles down her cheek in a caress that made her eyes flutter closed. The bitter-sweet awareness of her own desire made her tremble. The traitorous clamour of her body, urging her to take what he offered and be grateful, rose to tempt her.

'I want you to be that woman, Tessa. You know we're perfect together.' One last bright flare of hope ignited as she waited for him to continue. Maybe she had it wrong. Maybe he was so used to discussing business, not emotions, that this was just his way of explaining how he felt.

'You will be my wife, the mother of my children and my hostess. I will give you the respect and care you deserve. You will have a generous allowance too, to use as you wish, so you can feel completely secure.'

Tessa concentrated on breathing through the lacerating pain that tore at her as his words confirmed her fear. He wanted her because she was *convenient*. That was all.

It was strange how dreams could shatter and one foolish heart break, all in absolute silence.

A shadow passed over Stavros as he watched Tessa's face. Her eyes were closed, as so often while he stroked her cheek. That was one of the things he liked about her, her intense physical responsiveness to his lightest caress.

But it wasn't ecstasy he read in her features.

Suddenly, in an unaccustomed jangle of nervousness, he realised how desperately he wanted to hear her agree. To have her assent to his plan, her soft lips forming the word he most wanted to hear.

Strange that, in all his planning, he'd never considered the importance of hearing her say 'yes'. It was a foregone conclusion, but still…

Obviously years of concluding deals with water-tight agreements had him wanting closure.

But when she opened her eyes he realised something was wrong. Even in the soft light he could see the strange, unfocused look in her eyes. The tiny furrows that drew her forehead tight hinted at pain. His hand, as he moved to cup her jaw and splay his fingers over her neck, registered a definite tremor.

'Tessa! What is it? Are you unwell?'

Mutely she stared up at him and anxiety coursed through his bloodstream. Her skin had paled and he could hear her soft, uneven breathing, as if it cost her an effort just to inhale and exhale. He lifted his other hand to her shoulder, to curve round her slim back and pull her close. She was rigid beneath his touch.

'Are you in pain?'

Slowly she nodded. 'I'm sorry. I suddenly don't feel very well.'

That was some understatement. Judging by the taut way she held herself and the pain marking her features, she was suffering. Stavros remembered the stoic way she'd brushed aside her earlier illness, insisting that she was perfectly healthy, despite the medical report to the contrary. An icy hand reached out and clenched hard round his heart.

'Don't talk. I'll take you in and we'll call a doctor.' He'd stood and scooped her close in his arms as he spoke. His anxiety intensified at the way she held herself stiff in his arms, as if trying to curl into a ball.

'It's all right,' she lied, lifting a hand to shield her eyes against the outdoor lights as they approached the terrace. 'It's just a sudden headache. I'll be OK if I rest quietly, alone.'

Rest certainly, but not alone. Not when she was hurting like this.

Why hadn't he noticed her symptoms earlier? Because he was too absorbed in what he had to tell her? But, casting his mind back, he couldn't recall any hint of the pain to come. Only moments earlier she'd been smiling up at him with such sweetness that he felt like a kid who'd had all his Christmases come at once. The excitement, the pleasure, the satisfaction of knowing this was absolutely the right decision for them both. When she looked at him that way he felt something he'd never experienced before. A tenderness, a power, a longing, so strong it rocked him.

He'd barely been able to control the impulse to reach out and haul her up against him. Instead he'd had to remain aloof, not touching her until he trusted himself to take her hand without dragging her fully into his embrace and ravishing her then and there.

She shivered in his arms, her hand still hiding her eyes. But he could see her mouth, drawn tight in anguish, her bottom lip caught by her teeth.

So swift, so devastating. It must be a migraine.

'Shh, little one. We're almost there. Soon you can lie down in your own bed.'

Tessa didn't respond except for the hint of a nod against his chest. It scared him to see her like this. Never before had she seemed so small and frail. Even the night she'd appeared at the villa, almost collapsing with exhaustion, she'd been spitting fire at him, all defiance and flashing bright eyes. Watching her now made something inside him shrivel up in fear.

An hour later Tessa lay in Stavros' huge, comfortable bed. He'd ignored her pleas to let her sleep in another room, declaring instead that if he agreed not to call a doctor, she at least needed to be within earshot in case she got worse in the night.

The concern in his clouded eyes was almost her undoing as she sought not to sob her heartache out loud. She couldn't tell him there was no headache, but instead the shredding pain of her wounded heart.

So she'd let him give her a painkiller, strip her clothes away and cover her gently in one of his oversized cotton T-shirts. He'd bathed her face, settled her in the bed and slid in behind her, pulling her tenderly into his embrace, against the comforting rhythm of his heart.

She wanted to hate him for what he'd done to her.

He hadn't a clue that she loved him. He thought, stupid man, that marriage was about convenience, not love. He thought he'd found a neat solution that would suit them both. If he believed that, it was clear he had absolutely no idea what it meant to be in love himself.

Yet how could she hate a man who treated her like the most precious thing on this earth, worried and cared for her, even when he didn't love her? His strongly protective instinct was part of what made him so special.

How could she *not* love this man?

But she'd been wrong before. No way could she stay with Stavros knowing he couldn't offer her love.

She had to get away.

CHAPTER FOURTEEN

STAVROS looked at his watch again. The formalities should be over soon and he could return to check on Tessa.

Originally he'd intended to bring her here to the celebrations on the opening of the new school library. It would have been a good way to begin easing her into the local community. Though, from the comments he'd received, it seemed half the local matrons had found an excuse to visit his housekeeper lately, and to size up his wife in the process.

All approved of what they'd found.

As they should. Tessa would fit in anywhere, be it at a school fair, entertaining his friends at the small dinner party he'd organised for next week, or keeping his father amused. But most of all, she fitted in *his* life. In fact she seemed to have taken it over. He found it difficult to think of anything but her. Especially since she was still pinched and pale this morning, obviously feeling the after-effects of last night's headache.

The last speech ended, the applause died and, after the obligatory farewells, Stavros murmured his excuses.

He noticed the arch looks and the speculative murmurs. These were his people and they'd accepted both the dramatic end to his betrothal and the news of his marriage with barely a ripple, though behind the scenes no doubt tongues still wagged. Right now they'd assume he was leaving early to be with his pretty young wife. *They'd be right.*

He suppressed a grin as he strode to the car. He'd never looked forward to going home as much as he did now; knowing Tessa was there, waiting for him.

He felt Petros' eyes on him in the rear-vision mirror as the car pulled out onto the road that led over the hills to the villa. Instantly, and for no good reason, anxiety punched hard in his stomach.

'What's wrong?'

'It's Kyria Denakis. You know she went to visit your father this morning?'

Stavros shrugged. 'She often visits my father.' And if she was up and about that meant she'd shrugged off the headache completely.

'Dimitri reported that she had her luggage with her. Her backpack. He was told not to wait for her return.'

What? Stavros braced himself against the seat as the air sucked out of his lungs in a whoosh of disbelief.

'Are you sure?' Stupid question.

'Yes, *kyrie*. Absolutely sure. Dimitri called me.'

Blood pounded an urgent rhythm in Stavros' ears and his pulse ratcheted up to a frenetic beat.

'We'll call in at my father's house on the way home,' he said, then sat back, crossing his arms tight across his pounding chest. What the hell was she up to? And why did she need her luggage?

Four hours later Stavros paced the bedroom in the vain hope that *this* time he'd find something, *anything,* that could explain Tessa's flight.

For flight it had been. She'd left everything behind except for the few shabby clothes she'd worn when she arrived. She'd even left the Denakis emerald. The pendant that had so obviously enchanted her last night. The pendant that might have been designed for her.

His stomach cramped at the memory of her at dinner last night, so heartbreakingly lovely. One minute aglow with happiness, the next white with pain.

Fear shuddered through him. Was she sick? What if she was ill, alone, with no one to care for her?

He gripped the velvet jewel case tight in his hands, as if somehow he could wrench Tessa's secrets from it.

Why had she left?

Why *now,* when everything was so perfect between them?

Sto Diavolo! He hadn't realised exactly *how* perfect until he'd come home to an empty house and no hint as to why she'd left or where she'd gone.

His father had been no help, merely telling him his wife had every right to travel if she wanted to, and then berating him for holding her passport all this time. As if he'd needed a passport to keep her here, when there was such passion between them! She'd stayed of her own free will, of course she had.

Stavros turned and paced back to the window, crushing the pathetic hope that when he reached it he'd see Tessa out in the villa gardens. Here, where she belonged.

But there was no chance of that.

His father's words echoed in his head, like a recording he couldn't stop or erase.

'She's left you. Gone back to Australia.'

The old man hadn't even the decency to pretend he regretted helping her leave the island.

Far worse, though, was the punch of guilt and the raw scouring pain of knowing she'd left in tears. So upset that she'd been barely coherent. *Desperate. Frantic,* his father had said.

Slamming the jewel case down on the window sill, Stavros stared out across the gardens and the bay to the dark, smudged shadow of the mainland in the distance. Once they picked up her trail he'd follow her there.

It was taking all his resolve to stay here, do the sensible thing and wait for news. He wanted to be out there, looking for her himself. Yet if she called he wanted to be here to speak to her.

Why had she gone?

He'd offered her everything she wanted. Safety, security, financial certainty. A family, an indulgent husband, a physical intimacy he *knew* she revelled in as much as he did.

Stavros rubbed his hot, gritty eyes then thrust his fingers through his hair, desperately wondering what it was he'd missed.

There'd been no visitors, no phone calls or letters this morning. She hadn't logged on to the computer. So whatever had caused her flight, it wasn't news she'd received today.

He swung round and strode for the door, too wired to stay here, waiting for news.

Impossible that his staff hadn't yet picked up a trace of her.

As soon as the Australian embassy opened tomorrow he'd be there, waiting. He'd plant himself where she couldn't avoid him. She had nowhere else to go. He was certain she hadn't reached it before his investigators put the premises under surveillance. But how could he wait so long, knowing she was alone and unprotected in a country where she didn't even speak the language?

He catapulted out onto the landing and down the stairs, briefly checking his study for email messages. Fruitless, he knew. His staff would ring his cell-phone immediately they picked up her trail.

Somehow this one woman had escaped the massive network he'd mobilised to locate her.

Fear hollowed his chest as he drew in a shaky breath. The emptiness he felt inside terrified him.

It was more than fear for her safety. Far more than anger or pique at her departure.

He felt…lost.

Tessa woke to the caress of fingers over her hair, stroking down her neck to her collar-bone and out to her shoulders. The warmth of bare palms against her arms, the sound of that rich, mellow voice in her ear.

'Your cheeks are wet,' he murmured, nuzzling her throat, kissing her cheekbones where the skin felt tight and cold from the tears she'd shed.

One large hand drifted across the cotton of her nightshirt, his T-shirt, the one she'd taken in a moment of weakness because it still bore his scent.

'You mustn't cry, *glikia mou*. I don't like it when you weep.' This time the voice was stronger, firm with command, enough for Tessa to realise with a jolt of shock that this was no dream. It was real.

Her eyes snapped open and there he was, just a breath away. Stavros. Just like in her dream, only so much more spectacular in the flesh. The soft light of the bedside lamp illuminated the olive-gold skin, the gleam of black hair falling forward over his brow, the handsome face, the sensuous, well-defined mouth. Those clear grey eyes. Tessa had never read that expression in them before.

'Stavros?' She blinked. Impossible that he was here. He didn't even know where she was. Vassilis had promised not to tell him. How on earth…?

'Surely you knew I'd come after you.'

That look in his eyes clawed at her soul. So hotly intent, but so pained. What was going on?

She scrambled back, across the wide bed, and his arm fell away as he let her go. Tessa grabbed the cotton sheet and hauled it up over her breasts as she sat hunched against the headboard. Her pulse thudded hard and urgent as she surveyed him, the man she loved, sitting here on the side of her bed, large and real and utterly compelling with his dishevelled hair and his gleaming eyes.

She wanted to reach out and touch him. Her body cried out for him. He looked so wonderful in black jeans and a black pullover that was a perfect foil for the broad strength of his chest and shoulders. Instead she clenched her hands into tight fists.

'How did you get here?' Her voice was a thready whisper, thin with the emotion that clogged her airways.

'Over the fence and through the window.' He shrugged as he gestured to the sheer curtains behind him that billowed gently in the night's cooling breeze. 'I had the security code to silence the alarm, so it was easy.'

Climbing two storeys of sheer wall was easy?

'Why?'

'I had no interest in talking with my father again. It's you I wanted to see. *Alone.*'

Something dipped in Tessa's stomach at that last word, and at the possessive gleam in his eyes. She felt herself weakening, the urge to reach out to him strong and growing stronger by the second.

'Vassilis told you I was here?' How could he have betrayed her? He'd been so kind. No father could have been more caring with a daughter than when she'd shown up here, at his home, distraught and desperate for help.

'No.' Stavros shook his head. 'My father did his best to make me believe you were already in Athens. He took your side against me, his own son.' The silence between them was thick and weighty, as the implications of Vassilis' actions filtered into Tessa's confused brain.

'I knew he was hiding something, but I didn't realise it was you.' He reached for her hand then stilled as she cringed from him. She couldn't bear his touch. Not now. Not when she'd finally found the strength to make a break.

His face grew grimmer than she'd ever seen it. Each stark line seemed etched hard as if in unyielding crystal. She watched the muscles in his throat move as he swallowed before continuing.

'It wasn't till we'd checked every ferry, fishing boat and aircraft that I realised you hadn't left the island.' He bared his teeth in a semblance of a smile that made her shiver. 'I would have been here sooner, *glikia mou,* if not for that. Even so, I had my staff checking *pensions* and hotels in Athens when I decided to break into my father's home to look for you.'

Tessa's eyes widened. They were checking hotels in Athens? There must be hundreds, thousands of hotels in the city. The very idea of it was mind-boggling.

'I didn't take the pendant,' she said quickly. That could be the only possible reason for such a large-scale search. 'I left it for you on the—'

'I found it.' Something fierce and feral glittered in his eyes. 'Do you have any idea how frantic I've been? Wondering if you're safe? If you'd got into trouble alone?'

He had to be kidding. After what she'd been through a ferry trip to Athens was a piece of cake.

'I'm perfectly capable of—'

'Perfectly capable of landing yourself in danger!'

'Don't be absurd. I can look after myself.' She leaned forward, hands splayed on the sheet beside her for support. 'I kept myself alive for four years through famine and civil war, didn't I? I'm sure a trip to the Australian embassy is within even *my* capabilities.'

One corner of his mouth kicked up in a twist that might have signified amusement. Or pain.

'Do you have any idea how beautiful you are, *Tessa mou?*

I sit here and all I can think of is how much I want you. How badly I need you.' The half-smile vanished, replaced by an expression as sombre as she'd ever seen.

Tessa felt the impact of that look, of his words, in the breathless hollow that was her chest.

'Don't…' She'd had the strength to run away once. But to hear those words from his lips, read the wanting so clear on his face: it was a temptation no woman could withstand for long. She had to resist, to keep her self-respect and to find the resolve to start again, alone.

'It's true, Tessa. Absolutely true. I need you as I've never needed a woman before. I can't breathe without you. I feel it *here,* the pain when you're not with me.' He thumped one hand hard against his chest.

Tessa found herself leaning closer towards him, stretching out her hand across the sheet as his tortured look cracked her already bleeding heart.

'Don't talk like that!' She caught herself before her hand made contact with his solid chest. Welling anger warred with the instinctive need to comfort him. 'You don't *need* me. You don't need anyone.'

His lips thinned into a grimace as he watched her hand drop to the bed between them. 'I was convincing, wasn't I, *Tessa mou?*' He raked his fingers back through his hair in a gesture that said more about his frustration than any words could have done. She'd never seen Stavros look so lost, as if he was suddenly unsure of himself.

'*Sto Diavolo!* I even convinced myself. I can't blame you for not believing me.'

His hand, large, warm, engulfing, closed around hers and lifted it to the fine knit that covered his chest. His heartbeat thudded, heavy and agitated, against her open palm. Tessa's eyes widened as she met his.

'See what you do to me? What my own stupidity has

done?' He stared back at her. Gone was the arrogance she'd seen so often in his gaze. Now there was only pain and doubt. It was like seeing a man she'd never met before.

'I've never been so scared in my life,' he admitted, his deep voice cracking. 'I'm petrified you won't forgive me, Tessa.' He dragged in a huge breath that made their joined hands rise and fall. His heart thudded out a frantic rhythm of pain and distress that matched her uneven pulse.

'I don't understand.' She was too numb to work her way through this maze of strong emotion. 'I just want to go home.' She bit her lips on the childish wail that threatened to escape. This was too much, far more than any woman should have to take.

'I love you, Tessa. Understand that, if nothing else.' He lifted his free hand and brushed his thumb across her cheek, where the hot tears spilled anew. 'Shh, don't cry, little one. Don't cry.' It wasn't a command but a hoarse plea that only made the tears gather faster in her eyes.

'You're not in love with me. *I* know that.' How could he have fallen in love with her? 'You don't believe in love. And if you did, it would be with someone like the woman you'd already planned to marry.' Someone elegant and sophisticated. After all, just a few weeks ago he'd been planning to marry her. The idea stabbed at Tessa's heart.

'Angela?' His eyes widened as if in surprise. 'No. I was never in love with her. It was an…arrangement. We both wanted marriage and she seemed the perfect choice.' He paused, spearing a hand through his hair as if frustrated. 'That was before I understood about real love.'

'Don't lie to me, Stavros! It's too cruel.' She turned her head away, but his hand moved to cup her cheek and, lord help her, she didn't have the strength to pull out of his grasp. 'Just because your father told you how I felt. It's unfair of you to use that against me.'

'My father told me nothing, *agapi mou*. Only that you were determined to put as much distance as you could between us.' Startled, she looked up to see the truth in his eyes. 'The old man was so busy berating me for a fool that he didn't have time for much else.' Stavros paused and Tessa watched the convulsive working of his throat as he swallowed, felt his grip tighten on her.

'When I found you gone I was devastated. Only then did I begin to realise what we'd had. And what I'd lost. It took that to make me question what I feel for you.'

'I know what you feel,' she murmured bitterly over the sour taste in her mouth. 'I'm a convenient spouse. Just what a man needs to entertain his guests and warm his bed and bear his children.'

'Don't!' The volume of his roar made her flinch, but she couldn't pull back. His hold on her was gentle but unbreakable.

'Don't, *agapi mou*.' This time his voice was a husky whisper. 'I was a fool, an idiot, a biased, blind, bloody-minded bastard.'

Despite the string of emotions wound taut within her, almost to breaking point, Tessa's mouth curved at his choice of words. 'I couldn't have put it better myself.'

A gleam of humour flared in his eyes and then was quenched. His mouth was grim, his face hard as steel. 'You have every right to put it much more strongly. I treated you abominably and for that I apologise with all my heart.'

Her eyes flickered closed as he stroked her cheek and she gulped down on a knot of hot despair.

'Don't apologise. It's over now.' She couldn't sit here through his apologies. This was pure torture, having him so near, so contrite, so tempting. But nothing had changed except that he'd guessed how she felt about him.

'It will never be over, Tessa. Don't you understand? *I love you.*' Then suddenly his mouth was against hers, lightly brushing her lips as he spoke. '*S'agapo, Tessa mou. S'agapo.*' His hands, strong and hard and incredibly tender, tilted her head, fingers threading through her hair.

Ecstasy was a fizz of brilliance in her bloodstream, a burst of golden light behind her closed eyelids. Yet still her mind couldn't take it in.

His lips dropped to the column of her throat, pressing tiny, urgent kisses there.

'It will never be over between us, Tessa. Even if you leave me now, if you catch the ferry to Athens then fly to Sydney, I'll follow you. I'll be there, wherever you are. I can't let you walk out of my life and never see you again.'

His hands slid down past her shoulders to circle over the soft fabric that covered her back. She pressed into his embrace, giving him unfettered access.

'You can't?' Something had happened to her brain. It wasn't working properly. Not now, when he held her with desperate hands and told her what she'd so longed to hear.

'Open your eyes, Tessa.'

No! If she opened her eyes, it would be over, the final shred of this wonderful fantasy. It couldn't be true—

'Open them, Tessa. Look at me.'

Reluctantly she slitted her eyes open then widened them as she saw his face. He looked ravaged, anguished. Grim lines slashed deep, bracketing his mouth, and there was desperation in his eyes.

'I adore you. I want you to be with me because I can't imagine life without you by my side.' He drew a shuddering breath and for the first time she noticed the betraying tremor in the big hands at her back. She frowned.

Could it be true?

'I thought romantic love was a fool's fantasy. I thought a good solid marriage was built on…' His words petered out as his voice thickened.

'Logic,' she said. 'You thought it was about logic and careful planning.'

He nodded. 'I had no idea. I didn't understand that what I felt for you was so much more than desire. It wasn't till you left me that I realised...that I saw what I'd done.' His arms wrapped tight around her, pulling her close in his embrace. It felt like heaven.

'I don't deserve another chance after the way I treated you. I know that. But I'm not whole without you. That's why I'll follow you to Australia if need be and court you properly, as you deserve.'

'There's no need,' she whispered through the tears that blurred her vision.

'There's every need. Hell! I've made you cry again. I wanted to make you happy. I even traced your grandparents for you, because I thought it would help to know you have your own family.'

'My grandparents?' Tessa shook her head, trying to grasp his words. She was on overload, unable to process so much.

He nodded. 'The results of the investigation only just came through. Your mother's parents are alive and living some place unpronounceable in South Australia. You've also got two uncles, an aunt and at least a dozen cousins.'

Cousins? She had cousins?

'When it's time, I'll arrange the flights so you can visit them in Australia.'

Tessa looked into the dear, arrogant, chastened features of the man she loved and suddenly all confusion fled.

'So *we* can visit them.'

His whole body stiffened as if in shock. The only movement was the judder of his heartbeat beneath her palm as she reached out to touch him.

'Couldn't we travel together?'

'You forgive me?' His words echoed her own doubts of just a few minutes ago.

Tessa lifted her hands to his jaw. Eyes hot as embers held hers. She felt his uneven breathing on her face.

'I love you, Stavros. Of course I forgive you.'

The next few minutes were a blur as he hauled her close and kissed her with a familiar passion that made her senses swim. But this time there was something different. Something strong and true and ineffably tender.

Love.

Finally they broke apart to gulp in much-needed oxygen. Tessa sighed against his chest, revelling in his tenderness as he tucked her in close against him.

'You are a generous woman, *agapi mou.* So generous.'

She smiled, secure in his arms and in the knowledge that at last she'd come home. It hadn't needed the news of newly found relatives to achieve that. Just the love of this one, special man.

'But don't expect I'll make life easy for you.'

A rumble deep in his chest greeted her threat. 'I'll cope, sweetheart, so long as I have you. Already I'm growing accustomed to how *hard* things can be with you in my life.' The deliberate thrust of his body against hers told her he was taking a typically masculine, purely physical view of things.

She tried to repress a smile but she was too happy to manage it.

'I have plans,' she announced. 'I'd like to study.'

He nodded. 'Whatever you like.'

'And when I qualify I'll want to work, too. If I can. If I'm not too busy—'

'Looking after our family.' There was unmistakable satisfaction in his voice. 'Don't worry, Tessa, I won't try to keep you chained to the house.' His hand slid up to her hip, to linger at her waist. 'Though perhaps I'll be able to induce you to spend *some* time at home, with me. I've decided I need to delegate more of my workload.'

More time with her husband. It sounded like paradise.

'And I don't want you offering me some huge allowance I could never spend,' she added. His dismissive suggestion that she enjoy his generous pension as one of the perks of marriage still rankled.

'Of course not. That's all settled. I've already torn up that agreement you signed.' He sat back, putting a little distance between them so he could look into her eyes. His own were warm and loving. 'What's mine is yours, Tessa. You're entitled to half of all I possess.'

Her eyes rounded. He was serious. 'I didn't mean…I don't want—'

'I know you don't, sweetheart. So we won't discuss it again. After all, it's just money.'

Just money! He was one of the wealthiest men in Europe.

'Stavros, I—'

'Don't argue, *agapi mou*. It's done.' His hand slid down the T-shirt she wore right to its hem. Then slowly his fingers inched back up, this time along her bare thigh. Her breath hitched in her throat. 'But on every other matter I'm open to negotiation.'

His broad smile and the light of tender passion in his eyes made her heart sing. He was hers. She was his. What more could she want?

His hand slid higher and her breathing faltered. She recognised that knowing look on his face. Time to remind her husband that her *negotiation* skills were every bit as powerful as his. She slipped her hand under his pullover, enjoying the arrested look on his face, the tremor pulling his muscles tight.

'Perhaps I can persuade you otherwise,' she murmured.

'Perhaps.' His smile was ragged as she trailed her hand over his chest. 'Maybe you'd better detail your arguments slowly. One by one.'

1207/14/MB121

NEW from

MILLS & BOON®

Blaze

2 sexy reads in 1 scorching hot volume
ONLY £4.99!

From January 2008, Blaze will bring you two
stories in one super-sexy volume.

Look for
The Mighty Quinns: Marcus by Kate Hoffmann
and *Relentless* by Jo Leigh

On sale 4th January 2008

*Find new Blaze® 2-in-1 books at your favourite bookshop or
supermarket, or visit www.millsandboon.co.uk*

MILLS & BOON

MODERN

On sale 1st February 2008

THE GREEK TYCOON'S DEFIANT BRIDE
by Lynne Graham

When ordinary Maribel was bedded by handsome tycoon
Leonidas Pallis, she knew it was a one-off. Now he's back,
and it doesn't take him long to discover he is a father...

THE ITALIAN'S RAGS-TO-RICHES WIFE
by Julia James

Laura Stowe has something Allesandro di Vincenzo wants
and he must grit his teeth, charm her out of her shell and
into his bed, where she will learn the meaning of desire...

TAKEN BY HER GREEK BOSS
by Cathy Williams

Nick Papaeliou only dates impossibly beautiful women –
so why is he attracted to frumpy Rose? Nick is in for the
surprise of his life – for underneath her dowdy exterior is a
more alluring woman than he could *ever* imagine...

BEDDED FOR THE ITALIAN'S PLEASURE
by Anne Mather

Juliet Hammond may have made the biggest mistake of her
life. Raphael Marchese is like no man she has ever known.
But, because of the charade Juliet agreed to, Rafe despises
her as a gold-digger...

Available at WHSmith, Tesco, ASDA, and all good bookshops
www.millsandboon.co.uk

0108/01b

MILLS & BOON

MODERN

On sale 1st February 2008

THE SHEIKH'S VIRGIN PRINCESS
by Sarah Morgan

Karim, Sultan of Zangrar, assumed his bride would be gentle, obedient...but the one he got was far too headstrong for marriage and couldn't be a virgin! But Karim soon discovers she is entirely innocent...

THE VIRGIN'S WEDDING NIGHT
by Sara Craven

Harriet Flint turned to sexy Roan Zandros for a marriage of the utmost convenience... Now he's expecting a wedding night to remember, and is determined to claim his inexperienced bride!

INNOCENT WIFE, BABY OF SHAME
by Melanie Milburne

Patrizio Trelini is convinced his wife Keira has been unfaithful, and throws her out into the cold. Now she's discovered she's pregnant! Will Patrizio believe the baby is his?

THE SICILIAN'S RUTHLESS MARRIAGE REVENGE
by Carole Mortimer

Sicilian billionaire Cesare Gambrelli blames the Ingram dynasty for the death of his beloved sister. The beautiful daughter of the family, Robin, is now the object of his revenge by seduction...

Available at WHSmith, Tesco, ASDA, and all good bookshops
www.millsandboon.co.uk

0108/06/MB131

Coming in January 2008

MILLS & BOON
MODERN
Heat

If you like Mills & Boon® Modern™ you'll love Modern Heat!

Strong, sexy alpha heroes, sizzling storylines
and exotic locations from around the world –
what more could you want?

2 new books available every month
Starting 4th January 2008

Available at WHSmith, Tesco, ASDA, and all good bookshops
www.millsandboon.co.uk

108/06

MILLS & BOON

MODERN *Heat*

On sale 1st February 2008

BUSINESS IN THE BEDROOM
by Anne Oliver

Abby Seymour has just started a new business – only
she's been swindled. Left with no cash, she needs help…
She intrigues sexy, dark and brooding businessman Zak
Forrester, and he comes to the rescue. But, living and working
together 24/7, it'll be hard to resist
the intense chemistry sizzling between them…

MISTRESS UNDER CONTRACT
by Natalie Anderson

When high-flying Daniel Graydon hires Lucy Delaney
he doesn't expect much from her. She's the complete
opposite of him – flighty, carefree and fun-loving – and he
certainly can't work out why he's attracted to her. But
when one steamy night is not enough, he gives her
a short-term contract in his bed…

Available at WHSmith, Tesco, ASDA, and all good bookshops
www.millsandboon.co.uk

Celebrate 100 years of pure reading pleasure with Mills & Boon®

To mark our centenary, each month we're
publishing a special 100th Birthday Edition.
These celebratory editions are packed with extra
features and include a FREE bonus story.

Now that's worth celebrating!

4th January 2008

The Vanishing Viscountess by Diane Gaston
With FREE story The Mysterious Miss M
*This award-winning tale of the Regency Underworld
launched Diane Gaston's writing career.*

1st February 2008

Cattle Rancher, Secret Son by Margaret Way
With FREE story His Heiress Wife
Margaret Way excels at rugged Outback heroes…

15th February 2008

Raintree: Inferno by Linda Howard
With FREE story Loving Evangeline
*A double dose of Linda Howard's heady mix of
passion and adventure.*

Don't miss out! From February you'll have the
chance to enter our fabulous monthly prize draw.
See special 100th Birthday Editions for details.

www.millsandboon.co.uk

MILLS & BOON®
Romance

Pure romance, pure emotion

Outback Boss, City Bride
Jessica Hart

Needed: Her Mr Right
Barbara Hannay

MILLS & BOON®
Romance

4 brand-new titles each month

Available on the first Friday of every month
from WHSmith, ASDA, Tesco
and all good bookshops
www.millsandboon.co.uk

GEN/02/RTL11

4 FREE

BOOKS AND A SURPRISE GIFT!

We would like to take this opportunity to thank you for reading this Mills & Boon® book by offering you the chance to take FOUR more specially selected titles from the Modern™ series absolutely FREE! We're also making this offer to introduce you to the benefits of the Mills & Boon® Reader Service™—

- ★ **FREE home delivery**
- ★ **FREE gifts and competitions**
- ★ **FREE monthly Newsletter**
- ★ **Exclusive Reader Service offers**
- ★ **Books available before they're in the shops**

Accepting these FREE books and gift places you under no obligation to buy, you may cancel at any time, even after receiving your free shipment. Simply complete your details below and return the entire page to the address below. You don't even need a stamp!

YES! Please send me 4 free Modern books and a surprise gift. I understand that unless you hear from me, I will receive 6 superb new titles every month for just £2.89 each, postage and packing free. I am under no obligation to purchase any books and may cancel my subscription at any time. The free books and gift will be mine to keep in any case.

P8ZED

Ms/Mrs/Miss/Mr ....Initials ....
BLOCK CAPITALS PLEASE

Surname ....

Address ....

....

....Postcode...............................

Send this whole page to:
UK: FREEPOST CN81, Croydon, CR9 3WZ

Offer valid in UK only and is not available to current Mills & Boon® Reader Service™ subscribers to this series. Overseas and Eire please write for details and readers in Southern Africa write to Box 3010, Pinegowie, 2123 RSA. We reserve the right to refuse an application and applicants must be aged 18 years or over. Only one application per household. Terms and prices subject to change without notice. Offer expires 31st March 2008. As a result of this application, you may receive offers from Harlequin Mills & Boon and other carefully selected companies. If you would prefer not to share in this opportunity please write to The Data Manager, PO Box 676, Richmond, TW9 1WU.

Mills & Boon® is a registered trademark owned by Harlequin Mills & Boon Limited.
Modern™ is being used as a trademark. The Mills & Boon® Reader Service™ is being used as a trademark.